The Second Diary
by
Ciara Threadgoode

*There comes a time in life, when you walk away from all drama
and people who create it.*

*Surround yourself with people who make you laugh, forget the bad
and focus on the good.*

Love the people who treat you right. Pray for the ones who don't.

*Life is too short to be anything but happy.
Falling down is part of life, getting back up is living.*

by José N. Harris

This is dedicated to my mommy!

OXOXOOXOX

Chapter One
"My Gast Was Truly Flabbered!"

Dorothy Rose Nolte was born in her parents' handmade four-poster bed on April 1, 1936 in the small town of Truckee, California. She was the third child and first daughter of Preston Robert, my great grandfather, and Cherise Rose Nolte, my great grandmother, after whom I was named. I'm Cherise Rose Cones, or "Cherry," and I'm thirty-five.

My grandmother (Dottie, as she was often called) passed away in her sleep a little more than a month ago. Because her passing was still too fresh for my mother, and every other relative was amazingly too busy to help, my husband Gene and I were volunteered to clean out my grandmother's house and prepare her unclaimed belongings for an upcoming estate sale.

"We were thrown under the bus," as Gene so eloquently put it.

And honestly, we were. To avoid any family squabbles during an already difficult time, I agreed to do it. I was Granny's favorite granddaughter; she'd told me numerous times. Gene and I did visit her more than any other family members did. We were also the only childless married couple in my family and referred to as *"DINKs"* (Dual Income, No Kids), so everyone assumed we had nothing better to do than cater to all the family's unresolved issues. Not true. We loved doing what *we wanted* and the thought of a small human relying on either of us was terrifying. Our six dogs were our babies, but somehow that didn't seem to matter much to family members with babies of the two-legged variety.

During our first day of cleaning we found a diary under Granny's mattress. I remembered the book because my niece had given it to Granny on her seventy-sixth birthday, and at the time, I'd thought it was an odd gift to give a woman her age. My niece was tickled with her gift to Granny but I'd actually forgotten all about it until our recent discovery.

I thumbed through it and found it quite boring. She'd recorded the weather, a few recipes, and some random news in a prim and proper calligraphy, almost as if she'd known that the book would be discovered and read. I placed it in the box of things for my mother to examine, and then moved to a bedroom closet.

On the third day of cleaning and sorting, Gene found a second diary, neatly tucked into the linen closet, under a stack of pink polka-dot towels, her favorite color and design.

He quietly flipped through it before stopping to concentrate on one page. I was busy in the kitchen, working in the pots-and-pans cupboard, noticing that he had become extremely quiet, which he rarely was.

Suddenly he let out a piercing yell, "Eureka!", followed closely by "Cherry, honey, you've got to read this."

A quick peek at my husband, Eugene Thomas Cones. He doesn't get excited about the usual male topics. Doesn't give a rat's ass about sports. Doesn't drink beer or any other type of alcohol; refers to it as "milk of amnesia." Does not hang out in the garage, surrounded by classic cars, or collect antique guns and knives. Absolutely no fishing or hunting, as he wouldn't hurt even a fly; in fact, over the years of our marriage, he has prevented hundreds of insect deaths and is as eco-groovy as any one person could be.

Gene is into anything that smacks of gossip or celebrity or fashion. And the man absolutely loves clothes. No, he's not gay, although he truly fits all the stereotypical criteria. I've often told him that he'd missed his *gay calling,* although I am sure he is not homosexual. He's just built differently from any other guys I've ever known. He grew up in a house full of women. With six sisters, he was the baby and only boy. His father, his only male influence, was rarely home. He traveled and was gone most of the time when Gene was young. For me, his upbringing explains a great deal about the man he is today.

He loves *Oprah, Ellen, The View* and *Steel Magnolias* is his favorite movie. And *Judge Judy;* forget about even trying to talk to him when she's hearing a case. Does he like Judge Joe Brown? Not so much; another good indicator for me. He's also a real tiger in bed, so I know his sexual proclivities.

I didn't have time to set the armful of pans on the counter before Gene appeared in the kitchen doorway, book open, already reciting the passage he'd found so interesting and that had triggered his yelling for me.

I know because I placed a hand mirror on the floor, between my feet and slowly stood up, holding onto my walker of course, and there it was, clear as day, a bright red ring completely around my backside. His face scrunched up again before he asked me exactly how long I'd been sitting on the pot. Luckily for him, I had recently timed it, worried that I wouldn't be finished in time to answer the front door when the kids came. One hour, ten minutes to successfully make a poody-poo. I'll have to say that I was surprised at how large his eyes got. Big as saucers, they were. He scribbled down something on his white pad faster than green grass through a goose, and I handed it off to Cherry to pick up from the pharmacy. It ended up being a thick foam pad that fits over my toilet seat and a bottle of stool softener. My "gast" was truly flabbered. They have everything in those drug stores, from fly paper to toilet tissue.

Gene stopped and smiled his biggest Cheshire cat grin, "I can totally picture her doing this," he said. He was right; she was spunky. I reached my rubber-gloved hand out to him, asking for the book, but he turned, unwilling to give up the juicy treasure he'd found.

"You know how truckers keep two sets of books?" and he paused, back turned to me to keep my grabbing hands at bay, "to hide any extra travel hours from the authorities?" then he turned, his eyes sparkling with excitement.

"Your granny must have done the same thing! We found the mother lode of family smut," and then I became a little intrigued.

"You had me at family smut," I told him. Reluctantly, he handed it over. I flipped back to the book's beginning and thumbed through the first five pages. They weren't dated, but faithfully numbered. The entries were in sequence, starting with one and ending at 63, the exact number of days she'd lived after her seventy-sixth birthday.

At first glance, it was unclear on what day of the week the numbered pages fell. It also looked to be all random topics, unlike the first diary we'd found, with the weather forecast coinciding with the calendar dates. This was odd, to say the least. With book

The *Second Diary* 6

in hand, Gene and I finished up for the day, locking the door behind us.

I drove, as I often did, and Gene sat quietly in the passenger's seat, reading the newly-discovered book. Again, he was seldom quiet, so I took advantage of the moment and switched the radio on to my favorite station. A Nora Jones song, "Come Away with Me" was playing, so I sat back and relished the ride home through the beautiful streets of Santa Barbara, the American Riviera, as it is often called. It had been a full and interesting day to say the least, and I was anxious to get home and see my fur-babies.

Day One

Well I turned seventy-six today. Eight relatives came to celebrate, which is a pretty good turnout. The cake was cherry chip with dark chocolate frosting, one of my favorites, but not as delicious as cherry cheese cake. Cherry and Gene blew up several balloons and the dogs were all over them like a herd of turtles. I really enjoy those pooches. Peggy's not at all crazy about the hairy critters but it was my party and I invited them. Heather's daughter gave me a diary and announced she also has a diary and so now she and I are twins, bless her heart. She is cute as a bug's ear. I can't for the life of me remember her name right now. Twins? I do believe she needs to take a good long look in a hand mirror though, or have her parents splurge on a stronger pair of glasses because I look like something the dogs dragged under the porch. The party was wonderful.

When everyone finally left, I opened the diary's cellophane wrapper, lo and behold if it wasn't really two books. I'm not sure she realized it, but it gave me an idea. I'm going to pull me a Bert; be a secret spy, and have me a little covert operation. One book will be the decoy, the other I've decided to have some big-time fun with. This is a wonderful opportunity for me to tell it like it really is, minus the politically correct fluff. In my own written hand, the family will finally find out where I hid all the bodies.

I've always believed that the smartest people in the world are those who keep their thoughts to themselves and do more listening. I believe loose lips do sink ships, and on occasion, just make people look sad and stupid. My relationship with Peggy right now is a good example of that. My fault and I'm trying to patch things up with her. My mother always said that all of us have two sides: one we present to the world and the other that screams out the truths in our heads. She also said that if you don't have something nice to say...shut your pie hole. We were always supposed to keep our truths to ourselves. Somehow, where Peg's concerned anyway, my truths spilled out onto the floor like a leaky bag of flour, and I have my pie hole to thank for that. I'm still trying to clean up that mess. For a while, I suppose I was just out of sorts with myself and it wasn't until Cherry poked her head in my front door before a visit and asked me, "Granny are you a good witch or a bad witch today?" I realized then, I wasn't the Crackerjacks prize I had always thought I was.

I snapped myself out of it real quick after that. Anyhow, I had a busy day and I think I'm going to do a little reading before I visit dreamland. I can't remember who got it for me; sometimes my mind is like a bowl of overcooked oatmeal and I can't remember mush. Sometimes, I think that's a good thing; sometimes not so much. Anyhow, I got the book <u>Gone with the</u>

The *Second Diary* 9

Wind in big print, which is my all-time favorite. My mother first gave me the book to read when I was just knee-high to a grasshopper. She said that Margaret Mitchell was one of her favorite authors, and she especially loved the story because it was published the year I was born. It was one of her many favorites she shared with me. The older I get, the more I find that it's less important buying new authors' books because re-reading the old ones is almost as pleasurable as the first time I read them. I find I've totally forgotten the plots and story lines, just like leaving the chocolate chips out of the tollhouse cookies. I guess that's a blessing? I'll have to ask Cherry who it was that got it for me so I can thank them. Cherry forgets nothing. Thank goodness.

Day Two

Today started out pretty well I suppose, until I remembered that I had a medical appointment, a checkup with my regular doctor. He's the main one, or the "hub doc" as I refer to him, and these days I have several different flavors. If I have an issue, I tell him about it and I guess if he doesn't want to deal with it, he sends me to another doctor. I now have so many different doctors I can't *remember their names or what they're going to see me about. Cherry, bless her heart, keeps it all straight though. I asked Dr. Newman for a rather odd prescription today. By the look on his face, it was out of the ordinary for him, too. His face scrunched up and he looked at me with his mouth hanging open for at least a full minute. Because I was the one with the problem, it wasn't so odd to me. Now explaining it to him was a bit uncomfortable, but I figure he sees so many of us older folks on a daily basis, surely he only vaguely remembers me anyway. I know I forget him quite easily. He's not really that much to look at. I wanted something for the ring around my tush. Every day without fail, I have a nasty red ring that takes what seems like hours to finally go away. It's really sore. I really want the "ouch" to be gone. He asked me how I know that I actually have a ring, and I was truly hoping that he wouldn't make me go down that road, but he did. Telling him about it was hard enough; explaining how I knew it was there was just plain embarrassing, but I wanted that prescription, so I told him.*

I know because I placed a hand mirror on the floor, between my feet and slowly stood up, holding onto my walker of course, and there it was, clear as day, a bright red ring completely around my backside. His face scrunched up again before he asked me exactly how long I'd been sitting on the pot. Luckily for him, I had recently timed it, worried that I wouldn't be finished in time to answer the front door when the kids came. One hour, ten minutes to successfully make a poody-poo. I'll have to say that I was surprised at how large his eyes got. Big as saucers, they were. He scribbled down something on his white pad faster than green grass through a goose, and I handed it off to Cherry to pick up from the pharmacy. It ended up being a thick foam pad that fits over my toilet seat and a bottle of stool softener. My "gast" was truly flabbered. They have everything in those drug stores from fly paper to toilet paper. The only problem was when I gave it a try, my feet barely touched the floor. Gene measured the width of my walker legs and built me a little wooden step. That boy's a real treasure. Now I won't have that painful ring anymore and the dogs have another water bowl to relieve their thirst in case I forget to fill their bowl.   Let's hope Dr. Newman forgets all about that conversation.

Chapter Two
"Mad As an Old Wet Hen"

We pulled into our driveway to see six wet black noses pressed against the glass, smearing dog snot all over our picture window. Six butts were wiggling in sync. It made no logical sense to anyone other than us; Gene and I had moved the couch against the front picture window, giving our pups the ultimate view of passersby and other important neighborhood action. Front-row seats allowed them to spot even the slightest cat crawl or squirrel shenanigans.

The mail lady loved it, too. She often dropped dog biscuits in our front door mail drop, one for each dog, although I know for a fact a few of them were always left out because of the biggest piggy's scarfing up more than one in his little mouth. When Gene and I first met, he had a little long-haired red female Dachshund, Angelina, (after Angelina Jolie), and I appropriately had a little short-haired red male, Spanky, Spanks for short. He was a stocky little guy, built like a little brick outhouse, and from the day I adopted him until the time I met Gene, he was the only man in my life. As it turned out, we were both just weeks away from having our babies spayed and neutered, but we put it on hold during our courtship. After we married, we decided to have one litter of pups, and keep them all. That would be *our family*.

Neither Gene nor I was interested in having children, our reasons nebulous and plentiful, so the puppy plan was the perfect way of completing our special clan. I was an aunt to my siblings' children and Gene was an uncle to ten of his own assorted nieces and nephews. Just attending one of the children's birthday parties was both a chilling and numbing experience; we loved our fur-babies all the more.

We held a silly little wedding ceremony for our two adult doxies and while Angelina was in heat, we supervised their honeymoon. That was interesting and no picnic for any of us, either. I'd never seen breeding dogs do it before, and I'm happy to admit, once was quite enough. They gave us four beautiful pups to complete our perfect family. I allowed Gene to name them all, as was his desire. I waited with baited breath to find out the official birth-certificate-worthy monikers, or in their case, their American

Kennel Club registered names. They were Jennifer Lopez, Princess Diana, Brad Pitt, and Ryan Seacrest.

Right about now you're probably thinking *why is she giving us the details of her dogs' births and listing their names? Isn't this book about The Second Diary?* And the answer would be yes. But it's really quite simple. In order to decipher my grandmother's diary, any names, nicknames, and dogs' names will appear in the text, and without prior knowledge of this information, the reader might become lost and frustrated. For that reason I'm going to lay out as much information as I possibly can about everything related to my crazy family tree. People and places are named that I'm not even really clear about myself, requiring a little bit of research on my part, but I'll make a few calls or google a name or two until I have the facts straight. I'll get to all of that in a moment. First, I need to mention a little more about Gene and me.

My husband and I own our own small company, an Internet-only store, with a stock of crazy and unusual items, one-of-a-kind things found nowhere else. Gene did the research to find inventors and entrepreneurs willing to let us sell their cool innovations first. He's good at that kind of marketing. We make a fair living and run our business entirely from the comfort of home. The company inventory is crammed into our two spare bedrooms and one large storage unit a few blocks away. Besides the occasional trip to retrieve an item from the unit or to the post office to mail merchandise, we spend the majority of time at home. If one of us can't sleep, we log onto the computer site, wearing comfy pajamas. Not a bad deal.

This information will be significant because Gene and I, accompanied by our lap tops, spent a good chunk of time with my grandmother, as did our dogs. The year of her seventy-fifth birthday, Granny began having mobility problems. She was still *sharp as a tack*, as she put it, but her legs and knees began failing her as arthritis caused more and more discomfort. She'd also lost one of her dearest friends that year, which put her into a kind of depression that was totally unlike her once-bubbly, fun-loving character. I became concerned while my mother became frustrated and unfortunately the visits between my mother and Granny lessened dramatically. It wasn't long until it seemed like all the family had jumped on board my mother's train of abandonment and before you could say 'Jack Frost', everyone had stopped visiting.

Granny was well aware of the decline in family visits although for Gene and me it was a gift. We could visit and bring our babies without any family complaints, and my grandmother was actually pretty entertaining too. After some time she was actually a real hoot, but on to family business. As mentioned before, Granny's full name was Dorothy Rose (Nolte) Hughes. She was the third of four children. Joseph Robert (Joe Bob) born in 1932, William Robert (Billy Bob) born in 1934, Dorothy Rose (Dottie) born in 1936, and Margaret Elizabeth (Maggie Lou) born in 1938.

The Nolte children were raised in Truckee, California, in a two-bedroom house that my great grandfather built. My great grandfather, Preston Robert Nolte, or Pop as Granny called him, was the only skilled blacksmith and horse farrier for miles around. He worked from a barn built beside their modest home. Back then, even with gas at ten cents a gallon, the family didn't own a car.

They rode horses and drove their buggy to make infrequent trips into town. My great grandmother grew her own vegetables and canned fruit from trees sprinkled about their small farm. They raised farm animals, which supplied them with the necessary protein and fat. Every one of the children could sew, even the boys. Rarely did they go to the town stores, maybe once or twice a month, and it was considered a family outing. Pop often treated the kids to ice cream and gumdrops. The Nolte family was not considered poor by any stretch of the imagination, although my great grandfather often accepted items of trade for much of his work. From the conversations Granny shared with us, this bartering angered his wife, made her *mad as an old wet hen*. A real cat fit she'd have, she told us while stroking Jennifer's back, leaving Pop to mope quietly around the house for days at a time. No, they weren't poor, she emphasized. They always had enough food in their bellies, clothes on their backs, and a roof over their heads. Most folks weren't so lucky.

Day Three

A lot happened today. This is actually my second attempt at going to bed. Gene and Cherry took me out to dinner after a fast trip to the grocery store to pick up a few foodstuffs with a long shelf life. There was a big sale on ground black pepper that I just wasn't gonna miss. Bert never liked pepper on his food. He didn't like it at all. He just wasn't raised up with it was all. Pop often got a small bag of peppercorns among other odd items in trade for work he did for various neighbors back home. He was told that black pepper could cure things like constipation, indigestion, joint pain, and even toothaches. I don't believe there was ever any medical evidence of that, but I'm sure the man giving it to my father believed it. My mama sure hated it when he took the peppercorns in trade because it meant that she had to grind them. As soon as my oldest brother turned ten, the pepper grinding was passed on to him. It's funny how something as silly as pepper can plant a memory so strong, even digging up feelings of home and memories of childhood. Pepper is just one of the things that takes me back in time.

After our quick run to the store, Gene took us to his favorite restaurant. I'm usually interested in going home before I ever get to where it is I'm going, but the boy, bless his heart, is so excited about taking us out to eat. Gene at times is an odd duck, but my granddaughter loves him and he suits her to a tee. I think the boy's gay, with his colorful and exuberant nature, but Cherry says he's just an anomaly, very different from his quiet, reserved family. I believe her. He is colorful. The restaurant, however, was just plumb awful. First of all, it was so dark in there I came close to hurting myself just trying to follow the hostess to our table with my walker. I ordered the Salisbury steak, with the help of Bert's old Zippo lighter I dug from my purse just to see the menu, and again to verify that I'd gotten the right food. The steak was just nasty, like it had seen better days, but with half a bottle of ketchup, I avoided hurting anyone's feelings. It went down hard, like a lead balloon. But the French fries were tasty, and easy to find in the dark.

During the car ride home I could feel my stomach doing flip-flops, so Cherry fixed me a glass of Alka-Seltzer. Plop plop, fizz-fizz, oh what a relief it wasn't. All I know is that I went straight to bed after the kids left for home and sometime during the night, somebody pooped my pants. I don't know who it was, but I know they ate corn. I cleaned myself up and put my dirty sheet in the washing machine for tomorrow. Then I fished this diary out. It's now after midnight and I'm tuckered out.

Chapter Three
"Slipperier Than Snot on a Glass Doorknob"

My grandmother married Hubert Henry Hughes in June of 1952, when she was sixteen. The two had met at a school dance in town when Granny was fifteen and Bert seventeen. She explained that although she and her siblings were home-schooled by her mother, they attended the town's only school for extracurricular activities, which included field trips, dances, and a yearly spelling bee. My grandfather was originally from Santa Barbara but had been sent to live with his uncle's family when he was sixteen, after his family's home had burned to the ground. Because he'd attended the town's only school in Truckee, he also joined in all of its special functions.

It was at that year's first school dance that Dottie and Bert met and immediately became romantically involved. Both kept the relationship a secret until the day Bert's uncle took him to the blacksmith's barn to have some horses shod. It was then that Granny's father caught wind that his daughter was smitten with the Hughes boy and although he didn't embarrass them that day, that night at supper, while sharing the events of his work day, he boldly made a comment about the boy that had come to drop off horses with his neighbor, Paul Hughes.

"He may be Paul's nephew, but he's not from around here and if you ask me, that boy's slipperier than *snot on a glass doorknob*," he'd said. Granny ignored his silly judgments of Bert and began sneaking around to spend time with her new beau. On her sixteenth birthday, Bert gifted her with a silver band, also asking for her hand in marriage. The next day Granny spoke with her mother, admitting to her secret year-long courtship. After pondering her daughter's situation for several days, she told Granny that Bert would have to go to her father in the traditional fashion, and ask for permission to tie the knot.

They were married in June, the most popular time for weddings but not for reasons people might guess. Granny told me that poorer folks took their *yearly* baths in May and still smelled okay by June. She also said the whole bridal bouquet thing came about to mask the odor of those brides who weren't as fresh. The Nolte family did have a bathtub when Granny was growing up, and bathed once a week; everyone on the same day. Her mother filled the tub with clean hot water and in that same water all bathed. Her dad went first, then her mom, and then the children in their birth order. She said that's where the old saying, *don't throw the baby out with the bath water,* came from.

They'd had a small country wedding; her younger sister was bridesmaid. There were lots of lilies, roses, and gardenias, Granny remembered fondly; and her father gave her away. They lived with Grandpa Bert's family in Truckee for three months before moving back to his family's re-built home in Santa Barbara. A month after settling in, Hubert Hughes joined the military and that's when my grandparents learned that their first grandchild was on the way. Granny stayed with her in-laws while her husband was away at boot camp, but the couple quickly bought a small house of their own when he returned. Melanie Margarita Hughes was born in late fall of 1953. Grandpa Bert was often away on duty as a dedicated Marine and Granny said when he was gone, it was like a *dry peanut butter sandwich without her beloved jelly.* Undoubtedly she missed him. She single-handedly raised her daughter and the four children that followed. Her children were Melanie Margarita (Peggy, my mother), 1953; Reese Rose (Cricket) 1955; the twins Penelope Candice (Penny Candy or P.C.) and Brock Henry (the only boy) 1957; and Erin Jacqueline (Peanut) 1959.

In 1962, my grandfather was promoted to Master Sergeant and the Hughes family purchased a new home in celebration of his new rank. He was a real "Big Wig," Granny told me, and although I assumed she meant that he was somehow very important, I googled *Big Wig* later that evening. The term came from the eighteenth century when the most important men wore the biggest wigs. I guessed that the old term would now be equivalent to our modern day *my grandpa was dope*, or *all that and a bag of chips;* I'm not sure. My grandmother said many things that left Gene and me shaking our heads. It sometimes seemed as if we had literally been born into different worlds. She was certainly an entertaining lady.

My mother (Dot and Bert's oldest daughter), Melanie Margarita Hughes, married Harold Bryan Legg, also a marine, in

1970 when she was seventeen. Before my mother met my father, she went by her nickname, Peg or Peggy. Peggy Hughes is an okay name but Peg Legg, not so much. She soon demanded that all family and friends call her *Lanie*, and I totally understood her reasons, though Granny never did stop calling her Peggy. A poem was tacked up on Granny's fridge that I had all but memorized over the years, but finally took down and placed in my mother's box of Granny's belongings.

> *In search from A to Z they passed, and "Margarita" chose*
> *at last,*
> *But thought it sounded far sweeter to call the baby*
> *"Marguerite."*
> *When grandma saw the little pet, she called her "darling*
> *Margaret."*
> *Next, Uncle Jack and Cousin Aggie sent cup and spoon to*
> *"little Maggie."*
> *And grandpapa the right must beg, to call the lassie*
> *"bonnie Meg."*

From "Margarita" down to "Meg," and now she's simply

"little Peg."

This ditty was anonymously penned.

Soon after they were married, my parents bought a house two blocks from my grandparents' home and we visited almost every day, sometimes twice if we returned for dinner. Granny and my mother were like two peas in a pod, which made watching the distance grow between them in the last two years difficult to understand. Granny became a handful and as Bette Davis had so famously said, "Old age ain't no place for sissies." I often wish that my mother would've dug a little deeper and been a little tougher. It's my guess that now she wished she had, too.

My parents had three children. Heather Marie 1973 is now thirty-nine years old, Michael Scott 1975 is now thirty-seven years old, and Cherise Rose 1977 (me) the baby of the family.

I married Eugene Thomas Cones when I was twenty-two.

Day Four

Cherry called early this morning to check on me and tell me they wouldn't be over today because Gene was feeling poorly. She said that it might be a bug and she didn't want to give me anything. I didn't say so but it was my guess that it was the food he ate at that fancy restaurant. I wanted to ask her if he pooped his pants, too, but I didn't. It gave me the opportunity to wash my sheets with no one the wiser. It was actually nice being alone and flying solo today. I got a lot done.

Nora has been on my mind a lot lately and I wanted to dig around in the spare room and find a box of pictures I never got around to adding to a photo album. My friend might be resting in peace with a beautiful marble grave marker but not a day goes by that I don't think about her at least once. Ol' memories die hard. These days everyone puts family pictures on the computer. I'd much rather hold them in my hand and paste them in an album. Things have sure changed since I was a young 'un. Seeing all the pictures today made me a bit sad but also reminded me just how much fun my dear friend was.

Everyone should be so lucky to have that one special friend who is always there for you. Nora was mine. We met in the hospital the day of my first child's birth. She was brought to my room just as I was feeding my daughter for the first time. Initially I was a little upset that I had to share my room, but as the day passed and we talked, I was thrilled to have her there. We ended up talking all night long, the nurses chastising us more than once for not getting the proper rest. We talked about our families, husbands, and of course, our new babies. She smoked cigarettes and back in those days you were allowed to smoke in your room. Sometimes all I could see was a little orange dot across our dark room, our laughter bouncing off the walls. When a nurse poked her head in, Nora boldly reminded her that if they weren't in our room waking us for vitals every hour on the hour they'd have no idea we were even awake. That girl had spunk.

I grew to appreciate that about her, maybe even depended on it at times. I attribute a lot of who I became to my friend Nora. I was raised by my mother always to mind my P's and Q's and never be disrespectful. Nora taught me that while that was truly admirable and appropriate but one needs to be able to stand up for herself at times. When I lost Bert, she was there for me and I'll never forget the words she said to me during a grief from which I thought I'd never fully recover.

She said, "Girl, he was a better person because of your love. All we can do during our time on this earth is to stand tall and know that when we walk away from someone that their life was somehow better for having met and loved us."

I was sure better because of her, and my heart misses her something awful. She used to tell folks when we were out and about that we were sisters. It still makes me smile just thinking about it because she always followed it with, "She's my sister from another mister," and the puzzled looks we got were strange but heaps of fun, too. She was priceless, a diamond in the rough.

Day Five

Today I heard one of my favorite songs on the radio while out and about with Cherry. She had errands to run and I went along for the ride. When she ran into the post office, she left the car running and the air on for me and just as she disappeared *into the building, Helen Reddy's song "I Am Woman" came on the radio. I first heard that song at a karaoke bar several months after Bert passed and I believe it was right before we lost my brother Joe Bob. Nora talked me into stepping out with her, as she called it. I suppose it was better than bar-hopping, which I'd never done before. We'd often gone to the movies or maybe the mall, but one night she called and insisted we meet up with a group of her friends at a small bar called Sounds Good. A funny name, I know, but it made more sense when you got inside. It had a small stage and a big karaoke machine, a screen off to one side of the bar. It was ladies' night, buy one get one free, just the place for someone who didn't drink.*

Well I'd had two glasses of champagne only when Bert and I celebrated our last anniversary together, but other than that I'd pretty much been an alcohol virgin. Bert was the drinker. After about an hour it quickly became clear to me why all the gals were up on the front stage belting out songs at the top of their lungs. The seven-and-sevens with cherries really loosened an old girl up. Some of Nora's friends began flashing the audience from the stage, not a pretty sight to see; these women were as old as I was, but still funny as all hell to watch. I came close to busting a rib, I laughed so hard. Then some middle-aged man started hitting on Nora. She said the guy was so homely that only chloroform would've helped him get a date. She took care of herself just fine and the fella never bothered her again.

I finally got talked into getting up on the stage, joined at the hip with Nora, just before we left the bar. I was ripe for the Pickens by that time, with six drinks under my belt. We sang Helen's song, although she'd have cringed had she heard it. "If I have to, I can face anything" was my favorite line from her song. We had many let-your-hair-down nights, much to my family's dismay. My oldest daughter didn't catch wind that I was even going out until my answering machine picked up a call from her at seven o'clock one evening, well before she knew I turned in. She took a drive over and when she saw my car, she panicked and came on in the house using her key. She was waiting for me when Nora and I arrived in a cab. Peggy never much liked Nora after our karaoke songfest, but she didn't like a lot of the things I was *doing. I believe she first really started her dislike for Nora when her dad was still alive.*

Peg had decided to cook Bert some eggs while I was at the grocery store, rather than waiting for me to return, even though I tried many times to discourage it. He was at a weird, grumpy stage of his illness, the pressure contentiously building back up in his brain, causing him really hurtful headaches. I knew how to handle it and Peg just thought she did. She'd cut up left-over collards from the fridge and put them along with onions and cheese in Bert's eggs. He complained. When I got home with the groceries, Nora began whipping up some regular old scrambled eggs.

While we thought Peg was in with her dad, Nora said, "Just because you can put collards in eggs, doesn't mean you should. What was that child thinking?" Just as I began to respond, we both looked up and saw my daughter standing in the doorway. She turned, huffed through the living room, and slammed the door on her way out. I think back on it now, and I probably should have called and apologized. The girl was only trying to help by cleaning out any leftovers in the fridge.

Chapter Four
"Gallivanting, Letting Loose, and Partaking"

Now to finish up the last leg (no pun intended) of my researched information. The bad news is that Grandfather Bert passed away in 1991 of a service-connected malignant brain tumor. He was given six months to live but beat that diagnosis by living almost a full year. He'd made my grandmother promise never to put him in a veterans' hospital, and fulfilling that promise, she never did. Except for the occasional trips to doctors and two surgeries to release the pressure building around his brain, Bert took up permanent residence in the family living room, equipped with a rented hospital bed and round-the-clock family care.

Granny was a spry fifty-four or -five at that time so until his last days, she was his primary caregiver. I personally don't remember much about those last days. I'd been off busy doing what most fourteen-year-olds were doing, but my mother and Granny, still tight as ticks, seemed to have it all under control.

Near the end, I visited several times and saw hospice nurses helping with his care. I was amazed at Granny's strength and control in the days following my grandfather's passing, but my mother had said because Granny was relieved to see his suffering stop more than anything else. I believe that relief also rang true for my mother.

During the next five-year span, following the loss of her husband, Granny lost all three of her siblings, leaving her the last survivor of the Nolte children. Again, like a soldier, my grandmother held herself together with nothing more than grace, dignity, and lace-edged handkerchiefs. Of course she had her family around her for comfort and strength plus she appeared from the outside to be a poster child for courage, possessing genuine strength and perseverance. She kept herself busy *gallivanting* around with girlfriends to bingo and *letting loose* on chartered bus trips to various destinations, never letting the grass grow under her feet. She even *partook* in a sip or two from the bottle, again her description. She seemed to be enjoying life, enjoying everything and everybody around her to the fullest. It wasn't until her friends began passing away that her world slowly began shrinking inward, pulling itself more tightly around her with each and every loss like a net tightening around a school of fish.

She stayed inside the house more and her active thrill-seeking days diminished radically. She stopped driving at night, and then she stopped driving at all. At one point she refused to renew her driver's license, eventually selling her car and canceling the car insurance. The year of her seventy-fifth birthday and after the passing of her closest and dearest friend Nora, Granny became intolerant. Her personality changed noticeably. She was often snappy and bitter, like she had bees in her bonnet, but mostly with my mother. Her doctor suggested something mild for depression and before it was clear that it was even working, Granny stopped taking the medication. She accused my mother and the doctor of trying to drug her. She'd have none of that *wicky-wacky potion*.

That's the time Gene and I began visiting as often as possible. My mother seemed pleased with the news of our visits, maybe relieved that with us there she wouldn't appear to be abandoning Granny. She then stopped going to Granny's altogether. I don't fault either of them for the way things ended; I just wanted to be sure that my grandmother wasn't left to fend for herself. *In one ear and out the other* became our newly coined motto in those first few months. It helped us maintain our civility during the time we called Granny's *rattlesnake days*. After several long months, though, she actually improved. I believe we either wore her down or she accepted the inevitable. Gene, the dogs, and I weren't going anywhere, and no one else was coming to help us. My husband said she *chill-axed*.

A brief physical description of Dorothy Rose (Nolte) Hughes is relevant. She stood, and I'm guessing because I'm almost six feet tall and she came up to my shoulders, five-and-a-half feet in height. Her long, white hair was religiously kept in a loose bun, usually resting on the nape of her neck. She always wore a dress too, always looking *spiffilicious*. I'd never seen Granny in pants of any kind. Her dresses were always bright and colorful, polka-dots her very favorite design and they always rested uniformly at her calves when she was standing and just below her knees while she was sitting. She wore solid black knee-high stockings with black comfortable shoes.

Although her complexion was rather pale, she always seemed to have the prettiest rosy cheeks. Her build was medium and she often complained about her over-sized feet. They were larger than mine. All in all, she looked like a typical sweet old lady but looks can be deceiving. After the first few diary entries, one will have a better feel for this elderly lady. Bear in mind that Granny was the epitome of old sayings and illogical thinking, pretty much a run-of-the-mill grandmother.

Day Six

When I was young, we lived about five miles from town, far enough that my mother decided to home-school all of us. A smart cookie, she was. She went to the town's schoolhouse and got the lesson plans from the resident teacher and refined it to her liking. I know that we were taught much more than the school's required curriculum. My mother loved poetry, so we were given much of our English lessons learning and reciting poems by heart. I grew to appreciate it more as I grew older. One poem that she required us to memorize and recite for the family was "Paddle Your Own

Canoe," which has been revised several different ways and I hear now is even a song. I'd love to hear it someday. Maybe I'll ask Gene to google it for me. The poem was meant to remind us always to be self-reliant and mindful of our own affairs, never expecting others to carry our weight. No matter how forgetful I become, it's the one thing I never seem to forget. Thank you, Mom.

"Paddle Your Own Canoe"
Voyager upon life's sea,
To yourself be true,
And whatever your lot may be,
Paddle your own canoe.
Never, though the winds may rave,
Falter or look back;
But upon the darkest wave
Leave a shining track.
Paddle your own canoe.

Nobly dare the wildest storm,
Stem the hardest gale,
Brave of heart and strong of arm
You will never fail.
When the world is cold and dark,
Keep your aim in view;
And toward the beacon work,
Paddle your own canoe.

Would you crush the giant wrong,
In the world's free fight?

With a spirit brave and strong,
Battle for the right.
And to break the chains that bind,
The many to the few
To enfranchise slavish minds,
Paddle your own canoe.

Nothing great is lightly won,
Nothing won is lost,
Every good deed, nobly done,
Will repay the cost.
Leave to Heaven, in humble trust,
All you will to do:
But if succeed, you must
Paddle your own canoe.
~Sarah Bolton, 1851~

Day Seven

Well slap my chaps and call me cowboy, my son called me today, which was an unexpected surprise. He announced that he's coming to visit in a week or so, depending on when he can get away from work. He owns his own business but I'm not sure what kind of work he does. It might be one of those stores you can't walk into, the kind that's in the computer, like Gene and Cherry's. I'll have to ask him. I don't hear from him often enough. Peggy says that it's because he doesn't ever have anything good to share with family so he doesn't call, but they've never seen eye-to-eye.

I'm not sure if what she says is true or not but I do know that I don't always get told the full story from any of my children. They tell me only what they want me to know and think I'll swallow it like a glass of ginger ale without burping. I've come to depend on Gene and Cherry to spell things out for me. It's as if my kids coddle me, afraid that if I hear something unpleasant I'll self-destruct into a pile of ashes. Of course it's simply not true, pure hogwash. I'm tough as an old boot when I have to be. Brock does have an interesting outlook on life and a very unconventional lifestyle. I'm sure that there's much about him to which I'm not savvy.

He's been in trouble with the law a few times; he has a temper and when pushed, he acts crazier than a sprayed cockroach. He got that from his father and because he was my only boy, I probably allowed him to get away with more than I should have. If I could turn back the clock now, that's one thing I'd surely change and do differently. I truly miss my boy. When he was a small boy, I'd threaten to send him to the village of liver-and-onions if he didn't behave rather than ever physically punishing him by slapping him on the behind. He was my little man and the apple of my eye. When he started high school, Bert was home much more than he had been, shore duty; and when we got calls from the school about Brock's behavioral outbursts, Bert justified it away saying that sometimes trouble just follows a man. In hindsight, I believe he was just plumb rotten and we allowed him to pull the wool over our eyes much more often than we ever should have.

Brock left home when he was seventeen. Unlike his twin sister, Penny, he was smart as a whip and went to summer school to finish up high school early. Totally opposite from his dad, Brock very much disliked authority or being told what to do. He called submissive people robots without rhythm. When he had his diploma in his hot little hands he high-tailed it out of Santa Barbara with a group of his friends, ending up in a community house somewhere in the state of Oregon. He'd send me letters every few months, never a return address on the envelope and not one phone call. I'll admit I took his absence personally. It felt as if I was being punished for something I'd done as a mother.

Bert tried to make me feel better by saying that he was just out trying to find himself and men sowing his wild oats before settling down. If he told me once, he told me a million times not to worry about him, but I still fretted. Unlike most twins, Brock and P.C. were never very close, but he and Erin were quite a different story. I caught wind about a year after he'd left that he was calling her and often, so I did feel somewhat better that one of us knew he was alive and well. I'd also heard through the grapevine that he had been back to Santa Barbara twice and hadn't stopped by to see me. That stung a little, but I told myself that it might just be a rumor; like I said before, most of the time I was the last to know anything, if ever. I decided that he must have had his reasons if it was true and that helped me get through the sadness I felt in my heart. When Bert passed, Brock was the only one of our five children who didn't attend the funeral. He didn't call or send a card, either. I've never asked him the reason, but I believe I will when he comes to visit. Maybe I can fix whatever it was that I've done wrong. If it's got a hole, mend the tear and wear it again.

Mother used to say that being a parent is sometimes tougher than taking a bullet in the heart. I'll have to agree with her on that.

Chapter Five
"Ain't Nothin' but a Chicken Wing"

Gene and I love, love, love Costco. We go at least once a month and try to arrange our trip on a day that we can have Granny accompany us. I will never forget our first trip with her; you'd have thought she was a five-year-old at Disneyland. When she saw the aisles of books, I was sure she was going to squeal and clap her hands.

Granny had an absolute love of books that she's told me was passed on to her by her mother. She'd convinced us to go ahead with our shopping, leaving her alone in the fiction section to explore the extensive book selection. We honored her request.

When Gene and I popped over to check on her after thirty minutes of being left unsupervised, we found her sitting with an older, heavy-set gentleman with a big schnoz and a scruffy gray goatee. He looked to be several years older than Granny and they were laughing and chatting like they were old friends.

She introduced her new friend, Raylan, to us and satisfied that she was pacified and okay, we went back to shopping. A few weeks later my grandmother received a package in the mail with the return addressee as Raylan Stone. When I presented her with the package, the look on her face was first visibly skeptical that it was for her and then I witnessed a hint of true puzzlement. I wondered if she'd even remembered her encounter with Mr. Stone but before I had the opportunity to ask her, my husband began humming the song "Little White House" by Little Big Town and we both burst out laughing. Sometimes I don't know whether to hug him or punch him in the jowls. Understandably embarrassed by our outburst, she tucked the package down into the cushion of the sofa where she was sitting and began going through the other mail I'd given her. It wasn't until the next day with a good distraction plan that I finally found out what was in that package. It was a book called *Rootabagas Stories*, a book of fanciful children's tales by another of Granny's favorite authors, Carl Sandburg. I remembered this book as it had been gifted to me by my grandparents when I was young. My quandary centered on the reason why Mr. Stone was sending a copy of the book to Granny.

My curiosity was satisfied when I flipped open the book's cover to find a personally penned note from Raylan.

Rose,

I very much look forward to our date. It was such a joy meeting you, and like the old Persian Proverb goes, "He who wants a Rose must respect the thorns." My desire is to tend to you my beautiful Rose and to enjoy the luxuries of your warm silken petals while planting my seeds of joy within you. Because you should never put a whole loaf of bread in a toaster, I will visit a drug store and purchase the item you requested before our date. My heart is pounding just thinking of it.

Until then, Raylan

I slammed the book shut, replacing it safely in the dresser drawer in which I'd found it. Like Raylan's heart, mine was now racing, but I can guarantee not for the same reasons. Ewe! Loaf of bread, is that what old people are calling it? I'll have to admit that I never saw that coming. I quickly folded Granny's laundry, gathered up the two dogs that came with me, and gave her a hug and kiss on my way out. In that moment I decided that this was just one of Granny's secrets I truly didn't want to know about. I didn't want to ask any uncomfortable questions, but I couldn't wait to get home and tell Gene. She had given this stranger her address, and I'm assuming her phone number, too. So just how often after Gene and I leave is she letting her inner-bad girl out, and canoodling over the phone with some random gentleman?

Day Eight

Fantabulos, hellacious, pimptacular, bodacious, popping fresh, awesome possum, badonkadonk, and spiffilicious are just a few of the words that come out of the mouth of Cherry's husband on a daily basis. The scary part is I understand most of it. What he does to the English language should really be a crime. There are times when my granddaughter and their dogs are the only beings that understand him. When I first met Gene and I heard him slaughtering the language, I assumed he was two bricks shy of a full load, but the more I got to know him, I came to realize he was sharp as a tack and on point. He just likes to throw his own slang around, is all. Oddly enough I'm beginning to understand both him and my granddaughter though their new-fangled language just won't see fit to flow out of my mouth. It's like trying to put in someone else's dentures.

Cherry often says, "Granny drop it like it's hot," which translated means "Kick it into gear," which she also says to me and the dogs. She usually winks and then follows with a smile when she's addressing me. I don't complain. I'm too old to relearn the English language and because she's always been as good as gold to me, I just muddle through like a wet dog in a rainstorm. She's a hot mess as she often says about people she finds unique and a bit crazy. My very favorite is "Ain't nothin' but a chicken wing." I'm not exactly sure what it means yet, and I've never asked but Gene's usually smiling when he says it, so I assume it's good? They both tickle me. Today was Easter, but with my kids all grown it didn't feel any different than any other day to me. I received eleven Easter cards from my children and grandchildren and Cricket stopped by with a plate of food and a homemade basket, which I appreciated. I miss making baskets and hiding eggs with the children. Well I'm turning in now, big day tomorrow. The kids are taking me to Costco.

Day Nine

Today, and to quote my dear friend Nora, was cold enough to freeze the balls off a Christmas tree, so I layered up before I went out. It was a long but wonderful day, too. The kids took me to Costco that very much resembles an old hollowed-out horse barn, only bigger, with oodles and oodles of stuff. This was my third time going and I accompanied them in my wheelchair; we spent a good chunk of the day there. The first trip we made I couldn't stop thinking of my mother and what she would have thought of the store. She would have been tickled pink to have been able to purchase enough food items to have on hand in case of emergencies, especially when the critters or the weather didn't cooperate and ruined her gardens. Kids today just don't grasp what an old-fashioned hard life really was. Things are too easy for them now to ever really understand. Maybe if someone made a video game reflecting life in the '40s, some of us old farts could show them a thing or two.

My day started out great when the kids plopped me in the book aisle and took off to do their shopping. While I was there cruising the best sellers, I met a handsome man, who after just ten minutes of his compliments and sweet talk had my heart racing, my face warm and blushing, and made my knickers moist. I can't remember being as interested in a man since Bert, unless you count 2004 when I fell in love with a fictional character named Edward Cullen. Nora bought me the four Twilight books and when I finished them, we went and saw the first movie.

Much to our surprise, we weren't the only blue-hairs there, either. It broke my heart when I read the last page of the series, and I've reread the books several times now, since Nora passed.

I seem to remember a quote by Oscar Wilde saying that "If one cannot enjoy reading a book over and over again, there is no use in reading it at all." And that Edward was my kinda lad. Only this man Raylan is real; flesh and blood, talking and breathing. He had a cane but after the first twenty minutes or so of standing beside me, he went and fetched a folding chair from somewhere and sat down next to me. He was very charming, sweet even, but something in my radar flipped its switch and I decided to tell him that my name is Rose, which isn't really a total fib, but Nora always said that it's better to be safe than sorry with a man.

After the kids came to check on me the first time, I felt a bit more relaxed, knowing they could pick Raylan out of a lineup if need be. He is also a widower, and asked me if I'd be interested in accompanying him on a dinner date. As time flew by, I actually felt very comfortable in his company. What did I have to lose? I agreed to let him come and fetch me the next nigh,t and he jotted down my address before the kids finally came back to get me. Once they left this evening and I was all ready for bed, I began shutting off lights and locking doors. Raylan must have stopped by while I was in the powder room because a favorite book of mine, that I'd told him about, was on the floor by the mail slot in the front room. The note inside the front cover made me blush again but also excited me at the same time. It looked like I may have led him on a tad and given him the impression that we would be enjoying our after-dinner dessert in the bedroom tomorrow night.

I did say that these days it was a bit dangerous to date without protection, although I now believe that we might be on different wavelengths regarding that statement, but what the hell. This might just turn out to be fantastic fun; a ride on a carnival roller coaster. Hope it doesn't turn out to be the house of horrors. I have a bottle of perfume I've never opened. Tomorrow morning, first thing, I'm going to have to call Cherry and discourage their daily visit. I'll tell her that I want to catch up on my taped "Walking Dead" shows. They hate that program. I believe I'll stick the book he left me tonight in my pocketbook and return it to him tomorrow. I'd rather Gene and Cherry not see the note he wrote on the inside front cover. They surely don't need to know every little thing I do. Now I've gotten myself all flustered and the sandman won't pay me a visit. I need a cup of Sleepy-Time tea.

Day Ten

My goodness it's already three a.m. and I almost passed on fishing this diary out but changed my mind, remembering how forgetful I can sometimes be. I'd like to remember tonight for as long as I live because it might have been one of the most romantic nights this old gal has ever had. I'd had it all planned out to slip the book Raylan dropped in my mail slot under the seat of his car; I'd played my sneaky plan over several times in my head beforehand so as not to get caught when out of the blue he threw me a curve ball at the last minute. He announced that rather than go out to a restaurant tonight we were going to his place for a homemade meal he'd prepared. It seems Raylan is handier than a pocket on a shirt. The biggest surprise of the evening was that he lives just six blocks from me. My "gast" was flabbered again.

I kept the book hidden in my pocketbook, knowing that I could find a much better place for it in his home. Come hell or high water, I was going to get that book somewhere far away from my kinfolks' judging eyes. It was my mission. Raylan's words inside that book were like flies in my reputation's ointment that I didn't want spread about, mucking up the works. I decided to wear the beautiful new dress Cricket made me for my birthday. I absolutely loved the colors, too, pastel pink cotton with all different sizes of bright pink polka-dots, my favorite pattern. I ditched my walker, trading it for Bert's old silver duck-head cane. A few squirts of my favorite perfume and I was ready for Raylan when he arrived at six-thirty sharp. Cherry, the little rascal, called to check up on me at five p.m. and I purposely turned up my program as loud as my television would go so she would assume that I was settled in for the evening. I surprise myself sometimes because it worked like a charm. She quickly got off the phone, yes indeedy everything went smooth as silk, just as planned.

When Raylan arrived, he was sporting a lime-green jacket, crisp white button-down shirt along with a bright yellow silk tie. My first thought was perhaps he was color blind, as my oldest brother had been, but he explained that the jacket and tie were a gift from his eldest daughter and that she had talked him into wearing it for our big night out. Together we were sure "poppin' fresh" as Gene would most assuredly have called us. His home *was just beautiful. It felt both comfortable and cozy, the décor had a little country flavor. Raylan seated me in the living room with adult refreshment while he disappeared into the kitchen to put the finishing touches on our homemade meal. A strong smell of bacon floated through the house and after five minutes with my belly rumbling, I decided to go see what he was up to. The kitchen was cute and homey but not enough room to swing a cat in, so I stood in the doorway several moments before he realized I was there.*

The walls were plumb filled with what looked to be a hundred different antique plates and saucers, wooden shelves held old biscuit tins and a collection of salt 'n' pepper shakers as well as vintage teapots everywhere. Homemade rugs made from plastic bread bags graced the hardwood. Raylan had set the dining room table beautifully with assorted flowers as our centerpiece. The floral smell mixed with the heavenly smell of bacon and Dutch pannenkoeken had my mouth watering like a leaky spigot. I ate enough for two people it was all so tasty. After dinner we slow danced shoeless to his favorite jazz record and soon after he slid my panty hose off with his teeth. The evening got hotter than two rabbits making babies in a sock. I very much plan to see Raylan again. He's leaving for a few days to visit his son in San Diego but we agreed to another date when he returns. I successfully hid the book under the sink in his bathroom. He'll never think to look for it there. Tonight was wonderful. I felt like a giddy school girl in love for the first time. A good night, it was.

Chapter Six
"Winner, Winner, Chicken Dinner"

A little more than two weeks after Granny's seventy-sixth birthday, my mother summoned her siblings, along with Gene and me for an emergency family meeting. Although I wasn't completely certain about the reason for the meeting at the time, I was pretty clear that my grandmother was going to be the primary topic. It had been years since I'd seen my Aunt Penny or Uncle Brock as they lived in different states and didn't visit often. Aunt Erin and my favorite Aunt Cricket both lived just outside of Santa Barbara's city limits and always attended our family celebrations. Penny and Brock were fraternal twins, but for as long as I can remember never were very close. Uncle Brock lived up north in Oregon and Aunt Penny lived somewhere in Utah. My mother told me once that her sister Erin and brother Brock spoke often and that she kept Uncle Brock up to date on all of the family happenings. She'd also said that all of his siblings were upset with him for not attending my grandfather's funeral. Although she'd never come right out and said the words, I did catch her say under her breath and away from any other listening ears but mine that it was Granny's fault her brother was so disrespectful.

It was clear to me that the two were at odds with each other and had been for most of their lives. More than coffee, tea, and wine came out of that secret family meeting, although the only one it was really a secret from was my grandmother. An hour into the gathering, my mother called for everyone's attention and the drama began. Thirty minutes into the meeting and things began to get heated, sort of like a pot of water beginning to boil. Gene and I sat back and listened as my mother began with her matters at hand. She wanted to place Granny in an elder-care facility and she wanted her siblings' blessings and support in her decision to do it. She stated that while living alone, their mother was at serious risk of falling, as her legs were only getting weaker as time went on. While the room was quiet, I sat a bit taller in my seat and wanted to speak up and disagree with my mother, but I felt a little intimidated by my elder family circle. That's when I decided that my husband would be driving us home and I poured myself a tall glass of wine to relax and uncoil my knotted nerves.

I continued to listen as Peggy spewed out false facts about Granny's state of health and mental capacity, but before I could muster up the courage to jump in to dispute what my uninformed mother was saying, an argument erupted between my mother and Uncle Brock. It happened so fast, I wasn't at all sure what exactly had sparked it. Gene and I just sat back in our chairs as Uncle Brock, in a very bitter tone announced his real reasons for leaving home when he was seventeen. He'd caught my grandfather having an affair and from what I could make out as the words flew back and forth between all of them, he'd thought that his mother knew about it but turned a blind eye and allowed it to continue. Everyone began rehashing times and events about which I had no idea, so I kept quiet and when I saw a break in the yelling, I jumped up and poured myself another glass of wine. Gene was in his element, for him it was better than any "Judge Judy" episode ever aired. The look on his face read "Winner, winner, chicken dinner," one of Granny's favorite sayings, and no sooner had I sat back down when Aunt Cricket began crying. Penny began yelling at Brock and before I could blink, my mother and Erin jumped between them before fists started flying like round one of a boxing match.

Finally, maybe feeling outnumbered by all of the hot-headed hens, Uncle Brock flew the coop, slamming the front door behind him. It was at least another five minutes before the yelling among the four sisters stopped and they noticed he'd left. Then all eyes settled on Gene and me. Talk about uncomfortable, and it wasn't the heat from the wine. I felt like someone with green stuff in her teeth and no one was kind enough to tell her. Looking me in the eye and with tears still visible on her cheeks, Aunt Cricket blurted out, "Cherise, you're with Granny every day. Do you think my mom should go to a home?"

Now feeling extremely intimidated by everyone's eyes locked on mine, I barley croaked out, "I don't think she'd appreciate being taken from her home," and instantly my mother's eyes were burning daggers into mine. I looked away and felt Gene's hand cover mine and give me a gentle squeeze. Nothing more was decided that evening, but Gene and I felt as if a line had been drawn in the sand and it was Granny, Gene, and me against all of them. It wasn't at all a fair fight with Sergeant Peggy leading the battle. She'd try again, and we knew it. War loomed on the horizon. Better check our ammunition supply and prepare for battle.

Day Eleven

The kids must have really missed me yesterday because they were knocking at the door this morning before I'd had a chance to change out of my bed clothes. I know that I must have looked tired because I was dragging like a sock half on and half off. I can't remember the last time I stayed up past "The Daily Show" with Jon Stewart. Cherry kept giving me suspicious eyes and I was truly grateful that today of all days Jennifer decided to be naughty and chew the tennis balls on my walker. It took the attention from me and actually lightened the situation I was afraid was inevitably going to happen. Gene yelled, "Jennifer let Granny's balls alone," and Cherry and I both let out a roar.

Before she could focus back on me, I excused myself and headed for my bedroom to change. Before I could get the door closed, I heard Cherry yell from the kitchen, "Granny, what did you have for dinner last night?"

If I've learned anything in my seventy-six years, I've learned that you either should be truthful or extremely quiet. Lies are just too hard to keep track of. I climbed into my bed and took a much needed nap. I'm not sure what time the kids finally left, but a warm pot pie was on the stove when I woke up. I seem to have dodged a bullet today. Tomorrow may be a different story.

Day Twelve

Today was a terrible day and I actually hoped my forgetfulness would kick in. Brock showed up for a visit as he'd promised but our visit didn't go well at all. He was as mad as a mule chewing bumble bees from the moment he arrived. I could see his ill manner at the front door and it didn't seem to improve after he sat down and I made him a cup of tea. He just kept fidgeting and I watched him struggle to contain the fire he was feeling inside his belly. He wanted to get something off his chest but it was clear that he was tongue-tied and wasn't sure of the way to go about it. Several times after a tad of forced small talk, we just sat in silence, with me waiting for him to say what it was that he came to say. I wanted to grab him and smother my boy with a long overdue mama-bear hug, but his body language kept me from doing it. I knew better than to poke an angry bear. If you do, you're bound to get mauled. I may not have an education past the twelfth grade, but I have learned over the years when to take a hint.

Finally, but before speaking his mind, Cherry and Gene showed up, causing him to clam up faster than a goose-necked barnacle. He was cordial to the kids but he remained chilly toward me. He left soon after, promising to come back before leaving for Oregon. I wasn't sure if he was just saying that to pacify me or if he really meant it. Time will tell. No sooner had the screen door slammed shut than Cherry pounced on me with questions, interrogating me like Sergeant Friday which was a tad confusing. She asked me if her Uncle had said anything to me about my moving, which he hadn't. Then she asked if he'd told me why he hadn't attended Bert's funeral, which was another no. I asked her to explain why she was asking; Cherry usually tells me *everything, but she would only say, "Granny, I'll tell you everything in a day or so." As I said before, today was a terribly confusing day. The bees are really buzzing in my bonnet.*

Chapter Seven
"Playing Patty-Cake with a Dead Mouse"

A couple of days had passed since the family-meeting fiasco and I finally got a call from my mother. She'd actually been diligently and feverishly seeking out senior-care facilities, rather than just pondering the idea, as we'd assumed at the meeting. She had it in for my grandmother and I honestly didn't understand why. She even told us not to visit Granny for the next few days, insisting that if left to fend for herself, she'd realize that living alone at this stage of her life was futile and that she was being a stubborn and inflexible old woman. In her very next breath, she went all cryptic on me and nonchalantly asked if Granny had been telling us any unbelievable tall tales about her. I'll admit that in person my mother has one heck of an angry glare that could gorgonize me instantly, but over the phone, not so much. When I pushed *end* on my phone after our five-minute conversation, I was out-and-out mentally exhausted trying to keep up with her curious but confusing games. If she had been doing this to my grandmother, no wonder Granny was depressed. Gene and I decided then that we needed to have a serious sit-down about the situation as soon as possible. We also needed to include Granny in our sit-down before my uncle or mother came to visit her.

Only two scenarios would stop Sergeant Peggy in her tracks. Either Granny came to live with us or we packed up and moved in with her. Neither option would be handy because my grandmother, Gene, and I are pretty set in our ways, but it was clear that a solution of some kind needed to appear quickly. We made a list of pros and cons of both scenarios and packed up things for the day and with the dogs in tow, we headed over to Granny's house. Sitting in a kitchen chair in front of Granny, who was perched in her favorite spot on the sofa, telling her what her children were planning to do, might have been the most difficult thing I'd ever had to do. Like a soldier, she sat looking me dead in the eyes as I spoke, and I watched hers fill to the brim with tears. She never blinked once until her bottom lip began to quiver and then she held up her hand to stop me from saying any more. I obeyed. After wiping her eyes with the sleeve of her pale yellow sweater, she gently patted Ryan Seacrest's head. The little dog gazed at her adoringly and crawled into her lap. Once she was composed, and a few fast dog licks later, she looked back into my waiting eyes. Gene stood behind me, his hands resting on my shoulders. What she said next was as permanent and life-changing as the first time you hear the glorious sound of a church bell. It could never be unrung or unheard, ever! I caught myself holding my breath as Gene gently kneaded my shoulders and I waited for something, anything really, to leave her lips.

"Cherry, I'd rather play patty-cake with a dead mouse than be the one to tell you what I'm about to say, dear," and she dropped her eyes from mine and gave Ryan another pat on his head. "I believe I know why your mother is playing her mysterious, self-serving games and I'm pretty sure it's because she's frightened that I'm going to tell you a secret only she and I share."

She looked up at Gene standing behind me, bypassing my eyes as if I weren't there. I felt a chill rush down my spine and goose bumps sprout on my arms like gooseberries. She was calm, almost unnaturally still, while Gene and I were dying of anticipation and suspense to know hers and my mother's secret. What she said next blew my world into another hemisphere, and I became sick to my stomach.

"Harold Legg is not your father, dear, and no one knows that but Peggy and me. I found out by accident, really, and your mother made me promise never to tell a soul. She named you after my mother in hopes of ensuring my silence, and until right this minute I've never said a word to anyone."

Gene's hands were now still but squeezing my shoulder bones way too tightly. All three of us just froze, with our eyes bouncing back and forth to one another. Then the phone rang and Granny and I jumped as Gene stepped to the little table across the room and answered it on the third ring. We watched as his eyebrows squished together like hairy caterpillars and then he shot me a nervous look before telling the caller to hold for a second. "Brock would like to stop by and visit with his mom on his way out of town," he whispered. I shook my head no without realizing I was doing it, and Granny spoke up in protest.

"I'd like to see him, Gene; please tell him to come over."

Gene looked at me for confirmation. I continued gently shaking my head no. This was not the time for my grandmother to hear that her beloved husband had been having an affair. One life-changing morsel of news a day was quite enough. I jumped up and took the phone from Gene.

"Uncle Brock, this is Cherry. Granny has been a little depressed today and is also running a slight fever, so this is really not a good time for a visit. I hope you can understand," and I looked up to see the confusion written all over Granny's face. "Yes, I'll tell her, and thanks so much for understanding." I placed the phone back in its cradle.

Day Thirteen

I had a doctor's appointment today that went pretty darn smoothly. I now only have to take five pills a day rather than the seven I was taking. Cherry let me out at the curb in front of the office like she always does and went to find a place to park. I have a card-hanger to park in the handicap spaces but she says that she doesn't want people who really need them to have to walk. That girl is a treasure. A gentleman in bibbed overalls helped me with the door. Maybe seeing him today in his bibs did it, but I really had Pop on my mind all day. I've been preoccupied with thoughts of him and really missing him. Pop wore denim bibbed overalls every day of his life. I honestly can't remember a day he didn't wear them. He was even buried in a new pair and a brand spanking-new white shirt. Pictures of my mom and us kids, along with goodbye notes and a few heartfelt poems, were tucked neatly into his pockets. They tell me I'll get to see him again someday, and I'm just not sure if that's true or not, but I hope so. He was a good man.

Oh, Raylan found the book I hid in his bathroom. Wouldn't you know it, Cherry handed it to me with the mail and I've had to hide it in my dresser until I could figure out something else to do with the darn thing. It was like a bad cold I couldn't shake. Raylan should be back from his son's this weekend. I hope he calls.

Day Fourteen

Maybe it's because lately I've felt like I'm getting closer to knocking on Heaven's door and I was just too busy when I was younger, not having so much time to sit around and think about things as I do now, but I'm a tad confused about this whole God situation. My parents raised all of us kids to be Christians, and that was all fine and good but as I got older I met all sorts of folks with all different types of spiritual beliefs. Over the years I've known people who were Jewish, Mormon, Buddhist, Hindu, Atheist, Islam, and the list goes on. Today I got to thinking about all of them and their passionate beliefs. So I'm wondering if when we die, do we all go into separate bins like the recycling containers out front and who's keeping track of all these folks? I wonder if all this religion stuff is just a way to give us some kind of hope that things will be better after we die, than our time was on earth.

Bert used to say that the Holy Bible was really just a bunch of malarkey; a huge fib, claiming that things had happened way back when science had proven it would have been impossible. He *said if Noah had had woodpeckers on his ark, it wouldn't have made it a mile. Maybe I can find out the truth myself. I'll get Gene and Cherry to take me to the library and I'll find the book in the fiction or non-fiction section. I'm not sure if he was right or not, but today it's really given me something to ponder. I wonder when an Atheist has to testify in court, if he still has to swear on the Bible. How would that work? Maybe I'll throw all caution to the wind and just go with being a good egg. It would fit right in with all those other religions. A good egg's gotta count for something, no matter what gate I enter. I'd love to see a velvet painting of <u>The Last Supper</u> with someone who represents all the world's different believers and religions and then me, the one good egg. That would be some mural. It's time to rest my bones. I've thought enough for one day. My head hurts the way it did when I'd be figuring an arithmetic problem back in the third grade.*

Chapter Eight
When You Mess Up, You'd Better "Fess Up"

To say that I was perplexed with my grandmother's confession would be a gi-normous understatement; but oddly, the revelation did make some things I'd felt over the years make more sense. My brother and sister have sandy blonde, thick curly hair and blue eyes, while I have chocolate eyes and straight chestnut brown tresses. My mother used to say that I look just like my great grandmother, for whom I was named. I'd always felt "off" or separate from my siblings; never quite able to put my finger on the reason I had an intuitive awareness or peculiar aptitude, that I was somehow different, sort of like being a Brazil nut in a bowl of walnuts. Now I knew why, but what did I really know? I had a father somewhere out there who might have no idea I existed, or so Granny thought. She wasn't always kept in the loop, especially where my mother was concerned; of that I was sure. Maybe he already knew me. Maybe somehow I knew him. Was he my parents' friend or a secret, one-night stand ?

I took the best advice my grandmother had ever given me. W*hen things are going south in your life, stop everything and feed the birds.* It may sound simplistic and silly, but it really does help clear all the gobbledygook out of my head. It was as if my life suddenly stopped and I'd pulled out a blank canvas to re-sketch my day. With each chunk of bread I heaved, a fresh brush stroke of serenity came over my day; a soothing color on the canvas of my mind. Maybe this didn't have to end badly. Maybe there was a rational explanation and my grandmother had just gotten it all terribly wrong. *My mother knew the answers, of that I was certain.* More than anything else I was afraid for Granny. What would happen to her when my mother found out she'd been betrayed? Would Granny be sent away because she'd spilled the beans? What would my father do when he found out my mother had cheated on him; or did he already know? Would he leave my mom? Would he ask me to stop calling him "dad" and make me call him Mr. Legg?

My head was spinning and to make it stop, I took an exaggerated breath and left my pity party. I hadn't noticed that I'd been plunking the pigeons on the head with large chunks of bread rather than feeding them small pieces. As I looked around, I noticed a couple staring at me. They must have been watching my aggressive bird-feeding style. Suddenly I felt embarrassed and picked up the remaining slices of bread and headed to my car. I'd thought this stop in the park would help me sort through my new, unsettling predicament, but I didn't feel one bit better. I needed to talk to Gene. He'd know how to help me solve this perplexing problem. He always did. A chilly breeze numbed my cheeks as I drove home with the windows down. I couldn't feel anything. When I was young, my grandfather Bert had shared an expression that until this very moment had never made any sense to me, but now it rang clear: "I was wound up like a coon hound trying to pass a peach seed," he'd say, whenever he had difficulty. I wasn't angry really, just a little scared and confused. I didn't know how this complex phenomenon would affect my life.

I didn't want to be angry with my mother; she was, in fact, the first person who nurtured me and taught me about genuine love. Since I'd first opened my eyes, she'd been my protector, the one who comforted me and made me feel safe. How could I disregard all of that now and question decisions that maybe she'd been forced to make? My heart felt squishy and my head was pounding like a jackhammer. I parked the car and quickly entered the house to find Gene on the floor with our six pups, all sitting perfectly still, heads cocked sideways, surprised and looking at me. Gene had a look of genuine worry spread across his face. I plopped down on the floor beside him and within seconds was covered with furry love bugs.

"You know I love you, right?" came softly from his lips. I hesitated for a moment as I turned to duck the six tongues trying to taste my breath.

"I know" and already I felt better. I was home.

Day Fifteen

What in heaven's name does P.U. stand for anyway? I've heard the expression over and over again throughout my life and I never thought to ask anyone what the heck it means. It's like that with a lot of things. I have questions I've never slowed down long enough to ask. What do the good people in China call their fancy dinnerware? I've pondered that a time or two. And what's the difference between "fancy" ketchup and the regular kind? Jeez Louise and Mary Lou, my list could go on forever. Why did my granddaughter Heather give her four children names that no one can remember? Her oldest son's name is Saxby? Then there's Apple, Rain, and the last one's name is so strange I can never remember it. She's the sweet child that gifted me with this diary, bless her heart. Why do parents hang names like these on their precious children?

I asked Heather that very question one day and her hackles burred right up. I dropped it like a sack of potatoes at the time but it didn't satisfy my curiosity one bit. I often wonder why my doctor leaves the room for me to disrobe when he's just going to give me a large paper blanket to wrap around me and ends up lifting and exposing my goodies anyway. It makes no sense to me. These days, my upper goodies closely resemble two stale Hostess Twinkies and my lower dessert, a half-eaten Ding Dong, although Raylan didn't seem to mind much. It helps when your partner doesn't have perfect vision.

And while I'm venting, what the heck do you call a male ballerina? My great grandson Saxby takes dance and I'm not sure what to call him other than the obvious, a boy in tight leotards. And why are dogs' noses cold and wet? Do prison buses have emergency exits so the bad guys can escape if the driver crashes? How do they cuff a one-armed man? If they cuffed his arm to his leg, do they carry him like an expired deer trophy? I suppose Cherry is going to have a bushel of questions of her own for her mom today, too. I hope that goes hunky-dory. I've learned over the years that "when you mess up, you'd better fess up." It's the fastest way, if there is one, to find forgiveness. Well the kids will be here early tomorrow, and I need to get some good shut-eye.

Day Sixteen

Almost no one is honest, tolerant, or complimentary anymore. I remember a quote by Oscar Wilde: "Man is least himself when he talks in his own person, but give him a mask and he will tell you the truth." My mother thought Oscar Wilde was the moon and the stars. He also said "The pure and simple truth is rarely pure and never simple." It seems as if people and things are going to pot these days, which reminds me, I missed my normal poody-poo today.

The kids were over briefly this afternoon but the dogs didn't accompany them so I knew the visit was going to be short and sweet. I didn't have the nerve to ask Cherry if she'd spoken to her mother, but from her demeanor I could tell she was out of sorts. At times I could feel a tension lingering in the room. In fact, I could have cut it with a knife, like a slab of fresh butter. It gave me the heebie-jeebies. Gene was quiet too, and he hovered over her protectively. I wish Cherry would have yelled or screamed and said what was on her mind because it would have been better than watching her pretending nothing was wrong and keeping it all bottled up inside like a shaken bottle of soda. At times she looked as if she were a bottle of Seven-Up ready to explode. She gave me a kiss on the forehead and I grabbed her hand before she could pull it away. A trace of guilt touched her eyes, but then she gave me a sympathetic smile that told me I wasn't the one causing her trouble. That helped. She promised she'd be back first thing in the morning with all the dogs and that we'd watch a movie together. Gene asked if he could bring me anything when they came tomorrow and I quickly requested a lemon-filled donut to accompany my morning coffee. He nodded, smiled, and winked at me as he closed the front door. I'd never seen him as quiet as he was today. They didn't share any news with me, and I wasn't privy to what was really going on between Peggy and Cherry. Maybe the less I know the better. It usually rings true for other family matters. Ignorance is supposed to be bliss but it seems to bugger me like a mad hatter.

I did decide to call Raylan before I changed into my bed clothes; he, at least, acted thrilled to hear from me. He'd gotten home earlier today from a weekend visit at his son's and had woken up from his nap just minutes before my call. He asked if maybe he could come over to my place for dinner tomorrow and I told him that I'd have to check and see what Cherry's plans were first. Right now, the last thing I want to do is upset her anymore than she already is. Maybe telling the kids straight up that I'm interested in seeing Raylan in more of a dating situation than a friendly relationship would help them be more tolerant of him and appreciate my situation.

Oscar Wilde also said "Some things are more precious because they don't last long," and we all know I won't be around forever. It's worth a shot. Yes, tomorrow I'll be honest and tell them all about Raylan and me. Great, now my stomach's tied in knots. I think I'll brew a cup of tea.

Day Seventeen

Today I was happier than a baby pig in mud. I still feel like letting out a big ol' happy squeal. The kids arrived early this morning with dogs and donuts. We were sitting in the living room with coffee; Brad Pitt in my lap, and I just came right out and told them about Raylan and my big date night. I confessed that we were doing some dating of sorts. Gene just sat grinning at me like a mule eating briars and Cherry mumbled, "Granny, you're going to be the death of me", but then she cracked a little smile, too. The dogs even seemed happy about the news; all of them wagged their little tails with enthusiasm.

Then the best part. I asked them if they'd mind staying over for supper with Raylan and me, and they both acted genuinely happy to stay for supper. Cherry asked me to call Raylan and confirm and then she scooted to the store to buy spaghetti and salad fixings. She even picked up some ripe juicy pears and caramel dip for dessert; a big favorite of mine. Gene helped me spruce up the house while she was gone. Raylan accepted the invitation and was at my house at six o'clock sharp.

Everything went off without a hitch and I believe both kids took a shine to Raylan. He was charming. After the dishes were done, it was around nine, the kids decided to head for home, but not before giggling at the door before they left. Cherry said something about bread that I didn't understand, but the evening had gone so well, I didn't concern myself at that point. Raylan and I retired to my bedroom and he didn't end up leaving until just after eleven. Now I'm sitting here reflecting on the evening and grinning like a opossum with a juicy persimmon. It was wonderful. It was a good, good night, a-a-h-h!

Chapter Nine
"Marriages Are Made in Heaven, But So Is Thunder and Lightning"

I never confronted my mother about anything my grandmother had recently shared with me. I decided to do a little research and some investigative fact-finding first. With Gene's assistance, I managed to track down several of my parents' friends who had mysteriously disappeared around the time I was born. Two families living in military housing had simply been stationed at other bases, one was now retired and living in London. We quickly ruled out both. The only male friend we were unable to find seemed to have vanished off the face of the earth. Although I didn't want to, I contacted my older sister Heather, to feel her out for any information she might unknowingly have to assist us in our search. She did mention that she had godparents she'd never met, who were listed in her baby book. She'd said that she'd asked Peggy about them and been told that the family had moved to Germany and was never heard from again.

My mother had also said they'd lost contact a year or so after my brother was born. Gene, of course, found this report suspicious. It wasn't much to go on but Gene and I worked diligently to find any information that would lead us to their whereabouts. Heather's godparents, Lucas and Tilly McCallister, plus Clayton Kearns, had mysteriously disappeared leaving nothing more than an invisible trail for us to follow. This conundrum only made us more meticulous and headstrong about finding answers. Gene suggested we look in my baby book, which I hadn't opened in years, and unfortunately it was packed in a box, stored in my parent's basement. This hurdle wasn't going to be easy because it had been stored for at least seventeen years and my parents were hoarders way before hoarding was a TV reality show. We weren't just going to waltz in and retrieve the box. I also didn't want to raise any suspicion with my mother, so we'd have to arrange the time of entry and have a solid plan to be sure she would be somewhere, anywhere, else. Gene suggested we ask Heather to assist in our little operation of *Get-Peg-Out-Of-The-*

House, using my mother's upcoming birthday as our reason for the secrecy.

Heather and my mother were close, and I knew if we offered to pay for the planned luncheon date, my sister would be onboard and jump all over it. Sis and I had been close years ago when she was sweet and considered a slightly naive person, in a genuinely honest and compassionate way. Then she married Jackson and under his influence she became a mean, rude, and judgmental know-it-all. A Clint Eastwood line came to mind: "*They say marriages are made in Heaven. But so is thunder and lightning.*" Heather and Jackson together were best described as a devastating tornado, in whose path no one wanted to be. Gene thought that they attended any family celebrations so they'd have a couple of months of trash talk, negative and judgmental gossip to throw about between them to feed their addiction.

We witnessed it on the rare occasions they were with us, so we knew that it was just their thing. Granny suggested their chosen lifestyle was different from anyone else's; they were vegetarians and lived their lives as if the world was out to get them, afraid of everything and they in turn assumed everyone was judging *them*, so they judged back. I didn't totally agree. Jackson exhibited all the behaviors of a narcissistic personality disorder, but my sister's co-dependency left her in total denial. Gene and I purchased a book entitled *Narcissism: Behind the Mask,* written by David Thomas, that probes deeply into the psyche of a narcissist. Heather became defensive after mysteriously receiving the book and took it to my mother, complaining that we were out to get Jackson; that we all hated him. Peg read the book and later told me it could have been written word-for-word, as a mirror of my brother-in-law's behavior.

Though we all loved spending time with their four children, Heather and Jackson, not so much. That's why I initially had reservations about involving Heather, but Gene reminded me to keep my eye on the prize. We wanted to discover my real father's identity and the circumstances surrounding Peggy's affair. Gene and I went by the Olive Garden to pick up a fifty-dollar gift card and dropped it by Heather's house before heading for Granny's, asking her to call me when she'd set up and confirmed a luncheon date with our mother. I'd told her I was making mom a surprise; a patchwork quilt with assorted material from our family's past; namely, curtains, old shirts and other assorted treasures that I found in the basement. She was intrigued and maybe even a little jealous that I'd thought of it rather than it having been her idea; but she was all in favor of helping me, which in the end was all that really mattered.

Saxby, Rain, Apple, and Seven were all playing in the front yard when we arrived and they surrounded our car, begging us to open the doors and let the dogs out to play with them. We hugged and kissed all four children, making a clean break for the house, every dog unmarred, accounted for, and locked safely in the car.

Each night before we left my grandmother's place to head home, I set the timer on her coffeemaker to start brewing at nine o'clock in the morning. She rarely woke up earlier than nine-thirty and would be assured a cup of piping hot coffee to greet her in the morning. We usually arrived at ten o'clock or shortly after and it was a fifty-fifty chance that she'd still be in her bed clothes. She often watched the shows Gene had recorded for her after we'd left for the evening. Each day I anxiously awaited her confessions about her secret relationship with the Raylan gentleman, the one with the cute little badonkadonk she'd met at Costco, the same one who'd sent her the book with the nasty little message inside. Each day, nothing. Maybe she was taking this secret to the grave with her.

Day Eighteen

Cherry, Gene, and all of their doxies arrived a tad earlier than usual today and caught me in my flannel nightgown and slippers again. That makes three times so far this week. Gene seemed to be wound tighter than an old Gibson guitar string and got right on his traveling computer as soon as he was in the door. I believe he had something on his mind. Cherry seemed in good spirits and the dogs were energetic little pistols, playful and happy, like they always are. Angelina had an accident on the kitchen floor but the kids took care of it in two shakes of a lamb's tail, like they always do. They love those critters just like they were real children.

Cherry asked me if I'd help her with a patchwork quilt she wanted to make for her mama, and of course I said yes, but her request did get me to thinking about a quilt of my own I'd made years ago that Bert had put away in the attic for me. I'd traced all of my children's hands onto pieces of fabric, usually a square of their favorite color at the time; which changed regularly and often. I'm sure I'd embroidered at least five handprints, five years in a row for all five of my children, which gave me twenty-five separate handprints if my memory serves me correctly. Then I'd taken the pockets from their old jeans and hand-sewn those onto separate squares of fabric too. It's been years since I've seen that quilt. Dolly Parton sang about her coat of many colors, but I'm sure my quilt would put her coat to shame.

I asked Gene if he'd mind fetching it from the attic for me and he said he'd be happy to first thing tomorrow, because he'd worn shorts this morning and there was no telling what was up in that attic these days. He was right; it's been twenty years or more since anyone's set foot up there. Then there's the whole "dirt" issue with Gene. He's always dressed finer than frogs' hair and I could tell he was going to do it for me, but it wasn't on his top-ten favorite things to do. I know he does a lot of things for me way out of his comfort zone. The boy is a treasure.

Cherry made me a batch of cornbread muffins with real corn and purple onions before they left. It was my mother's old recipe and they were mighty delicious. There's only one out of six left. I called Raylan too, before going to bed, but I got his answering machine and was dumbfounded to hear a woman's voice announcing that no one was home. I'm going to have to ask him about that. Well it's been a long day and I need to turn in before I get grouchy with myself.

Day Nineteen

Well today was chock full of mishaps. I had a little accident and then Gene had one too. I slipped in the powder room and Gene fell from the attic. Aren't we a pair? Per Cherry's request, I usually wait for them to arrive before taking a bath but this morning I woke up early, a little after seven, and a quick bath before my coffee sounded like a grand idea. I wanted to be all cleaned up and dressed before the kids arrived. Things sorta went south soon after I dropped my gown and went to grab hold of the tub. Next thing I knew, I was lying on the floor with my legs hitched up in the air, hanging over the tub like one of those women in Bert's old Playboy magazines and Cherry was squalling at the top of her lungs, "Granny are you all right?"

I'm not sure just how long I was lying there but she got an eye full of the birthday suit she'll be wearing when she turns seventy-six. Because I had a bump the size of a walnut on my forehead, she insisted that we get me dressed and to the E.R. to have my head checked out. I honestly felt fine, a little embarrassed maybe, but nothing hurt. She still insisted, so we went. The doctor dismissed me soon after an x-ray and the damnedest thing happened on our way home. Gene called on his cell phone and said he was flat on his back in my hallway, unable to move. He was on speaker phone and I couldn't help but giggle because you could hear him trying to talk with a pile of dogs all over him, yapping and licking. I snickered just picturing it, which wasn't at all nice of me. When she shut her phone off, that's when she made her famous statement I hear so often lately, only this time the words were changed up a bit. "You two are going to be the death of me," she said.

When we got to my house, Cherry ran all the dogs out for a potty and then slowly helped Gene into the back seat of their car. She sat me near the telephone and fixed me up with a cup of hot coffee, plus some saltines and told me tersely to "stay" until I heard from her. That's what she tells the dogs, too. Her exact words were "Are you pickin' up what I'm puttin' down?" and I've learned to nod yes.

She left me in charge of her doxie clan. We all waved goodbye as she scurried out the front door. My land that girl had her hands full today. What a mess. After three dry crackers, I decided that some strawberry jam would be tasty, so I went to fetch some from the icebox and I found some boiled eggs in a bowl, sitting on the top shelf. I peeled six of the eight and with twelve brown eyes glued to me, staring me down, the house quieter than a graveyard at midnight, we had us a little boiled-egg party. When Gene and Cherry finally made it home and learned about our party, they were not at all thrilled with me. It seems that you're not supposed to give small dogs boiled eggs. I had no idea. I was tucked into bed at nine o'clock sharp, given a pill to make me sleep, and told not to move until they returned at six a.m. Well, I could've told them that that wasn't going to happen but I went along with it so they would go on and leave. Gene was full of pain medication so I knew Cherry would have her hands full again tonight. When I was sure they were gone, I got back up and had me a slice of pie. It was tasty and she'll be none the wiser.

Day Twenty

My goose egg has gone down some but my arms and legs look as if a crazed tattoo artist went loco on a fair-skinned old woman. I look pretty bad. Unfortunately, making things even worse, the E.R. doctor contacted my doctor, who in turn contacted Erin and then Peggy, thinking I lived with one of them. Poor Cherry got a tongue-lashing from her mother for not contacting her about my accident when it happened. I understand why she didn't call; she was trying to protect me from my daughter's wrath. Peggy has it in for me and wants to take me from my home and lately, any dealing with her has been as uncomfortable as a train taking a dirt road to avoid traffic. Because the kids and I have been putting our heads together, at least now I understand why she's on the war path. For a while there, I thought it was just me going senile.

No mother wants to think that one of her precious children would be so cruel. I remember reading somewhere that "A single moment of misunderstanding left unattended, can be so poisonous that it can make us forget within a minute, the hundreds of lovable moments spent together." I believe that's true.

Right this very moment, I don't like my daughter, Melanie Margarita, one little bit. When Bert passed, Erin and I had some ugly words, she was stricken with grief and thought I should have done more for her father; that I should have put him in the hospital against his wishes; but I knew at the time that, she was just trying to justify losing her dad in any way she could. My mom always said that in your lifetime, you've got to eat a peck or two of dirt; so I put my own grief aside and let her vent. The next day she came to me apologizing and all was well between us. This thing with Peggy and me is really all because she's plumb scared. She's let a lie go on for so long that she's terrified it might cause her to lose face and maybe even her daughter, too. I think I know my granddaughter better than that.

For as long as I'd known Bert, his hero was always Clint Eastwood. Beginning with the "Rawhide" series on the television set, to every movie that man ever made, Bert would recite his quotes to all of us. At times I found it a little annoying, I'd heard them all, hundreds of times, but for some reason one quote just popped into my head and darn if it doesn't make me smile just a tad.

Josey Wales said, "Now remember, when things look bad and it looks like you're not gonna make it, you gotta get mean. I mean plumb, mad-dog mean. Cause if you lose your head and you give up, then you neither live nor win. That's just the way it is." I miss you Bert.

Chapter Ten
"Fiddle-Faddle"

Gene and I made a quick trip to Costco without inviting Granny and it wasn't for any other reason than I wanted to spend some *alone time* with my husband. My grandmother hadn't been any real trouble, so to speak; just lately a bit more exhausting than usual. Instead of my usual couple bottles of wine, I tossed a box of six in the cart and Gene didn't say a word. I rattled on about the conversation I'd had last night with my mother, concerning her mother and two solid aisles later, I realized that Gene hadn't been listening to a word of it. I jerked the basket to an exaggerated halt and just stood staring at the back of his head until he finally realized I was no longer with him and turned around and gave me his famous *What?* look.

"Did you hear one word I just said?" I asked heatedly. His guilty expression softened and the right corner of his mouth turned up.

We stood staring at each other for a few seconds before he finally said, "No, and I'm sorry; I wasn't listening. I was replaying in my head, the highlights of our fantastic love- making last night."

The angry look I'd been wearing slid off my face and I gave him a silly smile. He walked slowly toward me, his arms wide open and hugged me with all his might, right there in the middle of the canned vegetables aisle.

I held my breath to stop myself from blurting out, "Well, of course you can't stop thinking about it booger-brain, you were so hopped up on pain meds you had me in positions even the dogs couldn't have gotten into!" He doesn't drink. And rarely takes aspirin. Of course his experience was different. It was probably exactly like mine after I have a couple glasses of wine. I truly love my husband. All my new family revelations had been upsetting to him, too. I could tell he was being overly careful of the way he worded things lately, in hopes of protecting my feelings. He told me that he was clueless about what to say to make me feel better about *the situation.*

Gene had always loved my dad, Harold. He said he couldn't imagine what I must be feeling and because he felt as if he had to do something, he was searching painstakingly, day after day, for answers to help me solve my mystery. He'd even found a few *Clayton Kearns* on facebook and sent friend requests, hoping that something might pan out with one of them. He'd also suggested that we copy all the files on my mother's computer, the day we were there to retrieve my baby book. I wasn't completely comfortable with doing that and we agreed to talk more about it before we left for our house. I felt uneasy about invading my mother's privacy. It was like watching someone on the toilet doing a poody-poo. I'd be horrified if it was done to me. We loaded up the car with our Costco items and headed to the house to pick up the dogs.

On our way to Granny's, my mother called three times, all three calls went straight to voicemail. Since she'd learned of my grandmother's accident, I'd listened to her rant and heard more than enough of her lily-livered threats. She needed to chill-ax. Even though my grandmother wasn't completely in the dark this time, if she knew just half of what the good people who call themselves family were doing, or contemplating doing, she'd be crushed. Days ago, I'd intercepted a letter from Uncle Brock in Granny's mailbox. I hadn't opened it; I was waiting to get a couple glasses of wine under my belt first. I might then find the nerve to read it. Gene wasn't aware that I had it, and I was hoping to talk him into helping me steam the envelope open. It was something on my to-do list that I hadn't quite gotten around to.

I'd really been focusing on making sure I kept myself firmly between the evil forces and my sweet little white-haired grandmother. While she and I were waiting to be seen in the emergency room, she'd asked me something I couldn't quite shake from my mind. I was accustomed to all her crazy questions but this time she managed to throw one straight out of left field. She'd totally caught me off-guard.

In her most serious and sweetest face she asked, "Cherry, if you could know the exact day you were going to die, would you want to know?"

At first, alarms were going off inside my head and then my heart began pounding loudly in my chest. For an instant I thought maybe she was trying to tell me something; information I'd stupidly missed. But as I stared into her weary brown eyes and bruised face, I realized it was just another question she wanted help answering. I admitted I didn't have an answer for her. That I wasn't sure if I'd want to know. She seemed satisfied with that, but for some reason, I wasn't.

Then there was that whole Raylan thing, that at first I found several shades of creepy. He really seemed to make my grandmother happy, and after spending an evening with him, I decided who was I to tell her she couldn't spend time with a gentleman friend if that's what she wanted to do. I just had to be sure my mother or any other family members didn't find out about it. That would not be good for any of us. They already had enough ammunition.

When we arrived, Granny was perched in her favorite spot on the sofa, still in her bed clothes and slippers, sipping her coffee, looking very content. Her eyes lit up when she saw the doxies and they all piled up around her before she could set her cup down. Gene had never gotten that quilt from the attic; he'd slipped and hurt his back on the way up. She didn't ask anymore about it and because of all of the chaos that day, I purposely never mentioned it again either.

Day Twenty-One

Today I woke with the worst hankering for a chili dog with purple onions, heavy on the cheese. I told Cherry about it when she arrived and she said she'd already taken some pork chops out to defrost. Just when I thought hotdogs were off the menu, Gene piped up and said he'd enjoy some chili dogs too. Maybe it was because of all the smiling I was doing, but Cherry folded like a bad hand of cards and Gene offered to make a grocery list of what we needed and run to the store. That boy is a keeper. They were the best dogs I'd ever tasted. The company wasn't bad, either. We had root beer floats for dessert. Cherry told me not to expect them until about two p.m. tomorrow. I'll bet they have to tend to something at that store of theirs that I have yet to see. Who in the heck buys a store you can't walk into? It beats all but does save money on bricks and mortar.

Cricket and Peanut called today, to check in with me. Cricket said she'll come by sometime this weekend for a visit. Right this very minute, I look forward to that like a bad case of the flu. When I get to thinking about all the predicaments my children threw at me when they were growing up, I have to stop myself and remember what my dear friend Nora went through. That girl had three children that bled her dry. The oldest boy, Dustin, was the worst of the three; and the spitting image of his father. All Nora's children had different fathers but that Dustin was about as useful as a pogo stick in quicksand. He could talk an old woman into buying a heart attack from him but he sure couldn't keep himself out of trouble. Nora always said that the boy would be the death of her. It just tore me up to have to sit back and watch it sometimes and if I'd thought for one minute she'd have allowed me to, I'd have scooped that child up by his ear and given him a good scolding. Oh well, she doesn't have to put up with his bologna anymore, I suppose.

I called Raylan this evening right after the kids went home and we talked for a good hour or more. It seems that he's been busy with doctors' appointments. I sure know how that is. I have a check-up sometime next week about the bump on my noggin. I finally asked him about that female on his answering machine that I'd been wondering about and he explained that it was his deceased wife's voice recorded eight years earlier. He said that he just couldn't bring himself to erase it. I understand that. We all want to hold on tight to the memories of our loved ones. Actually, he was lucky in a way, because he could replay that message and hear her voice. I just had some pictures and a few letters that Bert had written to me.

Well I'm going to close for now. I'm too tuckered out to make me a cup of tea. I feel like if I sat myself down in a rocking chair I wouldn't have the energy to get the thing going. I should talk to Cherry tomorrow about picking up a bottle of castor oil. That always seems to put a bounce in my step when I'm dragging, almost like a kick in the butt with a steel-toed boot.

Day Twenty-Two

Back when I was a youngster, all of us kids begged to lick the cake bowl and never died from the raw eggs our mother had put in the batter. We ate everything from sugary cupcakes and loads of homemade bread with fresh churned butter, to even sharing a soda between us, same glass bottle and never once got cooties. At Easter we ate the colored eggs we found on the hunt, even though they'd been hidden the night before, and we lived to tell about it. We made up our own games with sticks or balls and we played by the rules that we'd all made. If you lost, you lost. No do-over could be requested. When we had fights we didn't run to an adult to settle them for us. We punched each other, sometimes even drew blood or got a fat eye, but we always settled things between us. Today's kids are like soggy potato chips, not a crisp one among them. My granddaughter Heather called me today, before Cherry and Gene showed up and was proudly boasting about her oldest son's little league game. When I asked what the score was, she informed me that they don't keep score. Every child was a winner, she said; they even gave every child a trophy at the season's end. I wanted to tell her that that was the most cockamamie thing I'd ever heard, but I kept my pie hole shut.

When my kids were young, Little League had try-outs and not everyone was good enough to make the team. If someone said a child had talent, it just meant that he practiced and worked hard to be better than the kids that didn't. Those who didn't work hard enough learned to deal with disappointment and either tried harder or quit. I wondered to myself while she was going on and on, if she honestly believed that her boy didn't know who'd won and didn't feel gypped that he had to walk away without a victory? Sometimes I think, though I love my granddaughter to pieces, that she's a couple pups short of a pet shop and she needs to eat a hamburger once in a while. I'm not saying that she's a bad person; I just wonder if Peggy and Harry skipped teaching their children about life and consequences. Instead, they were giving their kids video games, cable TV, computers, and cell phones. Mine didn't have all that fiddle faddle; they had real friends and after school they went outside and found them. They knew when the street lights came on, it was time to get their butts home. If *they didn't do the required assignments in school, they risked failing that grade and would be held back to repeat it until they passed on their own merit. Parents didn't do their children's work for them and they didn't entertain their offspring twenty-four/seven. Kids had imaginations and they used them. The world today is sure a different place.*

Cricket came by today while the kids were here but sent them off on a trip to the store to fetch something for her. What she really wanted was some private time with me. She asked if I knew where the paperwork to my house was stored and if Bert was still listed as the owner with me. I told her yes to both questions and then she proceeded to tell me that I really needed to get that all changed, which she offered to help me with, just in case something were to happen to me. I was a little puzzled at that moment, not sure of the reason it was so cotton-picking important, but now that I've had some time to mull it over, it's a tad bit clearer. She doesn't know I've been to a lawyer since Bert passed. None of the kids do. I just told her that I'd give it some thought and get back to her. She didn't need to know that Nora and I had already thought ahead. Nora was worried about her children, and said that her oldest boy would sell her cremated ashes if he was able; so I tagged along with her and got my own affairs in order too. I often wonder what became of her children. I hope they're all doing well. It seems I have a doctor's appointment tomorrow mid-morning, so I'd better turn in for now.

Day Twenty-Three

It's a tad embarrassing at the doctor's office when you start mimicking the noises your coffeemaker makes, while sitting naked on a table wrapped in nothing but a paper blanket. After excusing myself three times, I just gave up and let 'em rip. Everyone's heard the saying, "Beans, beans the musical fruit, the more you eat the more you shoot." Maybe eating the rest of the chili for breakfast, instead of oatmeal, wasn't such a good idea. I would've bet the farm I wasn't going to have to strip down for a follow-up visit for a bump on my head, but there I was, naked as a jay-bird. My doctor asked me how I'd been feeling and then out of the blue he said that castor oil and the medications I was now taking didn't go well together and would weaken the potency of some of my meds. I knew better. I'd been taking a teaspoon of castor oil for most of my life with no problems. Bikinis and liver spots, or roller skates and walkers didn't mesh, but he didn't know what he was talking about when it came to castor oil. Cherry must have called his office before I arrived and tattled that I'd complained about being worn out some days. She was sneaky like that. To my face, she acted as if together we were rebels, girl power all the way, but when I wasn't looking, she was doing a little motherly meddling. After a million questions, I was finally allowed to get dressed and he gave me two new prescriptions. I'm back to taking seven different pills a day. Whoopee! I handed the scrips off to Cherry when I got to the waiting room and I could see a little guilt painted on her face. I suppose I should be grateful that she cares so much about me. We stopped and picked up some burgers for Cherry and me and then stopped at a Mexican shop for rolled tacos for Gene. I ordered some too. I couldn't make up my mind which sounded better, a hamburger or tacos. The kids left early today and it's now ten p.m. and I'm thinking about a cup of tea and then hitting the sack. My left arm is giving me fits today and the Tylenol I took earlier isn't touching it. Sometimes I think my arm has a mind of its own and acts without my permission.

Chapter Eleven
"What My Name Spelled Backwards Says"

"Operation Baby Book" went off without a hitch. Well, except for the unexpected time crunch that we worked around. Heather and mom were supposed to meet at eleven-thirty, and the restaurant was a good twenty minutes across town, but when we arrived at eleven-fifteen, her car was still parked in the driveway. Gene and I did a quick drive-by and made a circle around her block. Peggy was always late. My grandmother joked that she'd be late for her own funeral and she's probably right about that. My mother made all of us late for everything when we were growing up.

When we finally went down to the basement, we went through boxes quickly and feverishly. I had drawn big red hearts on all sides of the boxes I'd packed and stored, just in case an occasion exactly like this one arose, hardy, har, har. When I'd left home, I wasn't on the best of terms with my parents. Being the last child and the baby, my mother found any and all obstacles that would keep me from leaving the nest.

There was even a bribe or two of sorts, but I was just as determined to leave as she was to have me stay and so I'd left in the middle of the night. Almost two years had passed before she forgave me and we established any real mother-daughter rapport. We really started talking about six months before I married Gene. During that time Mom and Granny were tight as ticks. Maybe that's the reason my mother decided finally, to bury the hatchet. Or it was Granny's insistence that she make peace. I'm not really sure.

Gene and I moved quickly, making a path to the back of the basement, where I vaguely remembered placing the boxes, years ago. Gene kept whistling "Secret Agent Man" and kept just far enough out of my reach that I wasn't able to smack him. We'd found five boxes, emptied them, then re-packed them before we finally found the one with my baby book. Carefully we replaced everything we'd moved, until it was exactly the way we'd found it, and headed upstairs to make a retreat. That's when Gene was going to make me push the envelope and make a decision about his retrieving the files from my mother's computer. Standing frozen in my mother's kitchen, we stared at each other. It was already one-thirty p.m. and if we were going to accomplish this goal, we needed to do it right now and lightning fast.

I took in a deep breath, looked into his eyes and whispered as I exhaled, "What the hell, go do it!" He was off to my mother's den before I could blink. With her files copied, we jumped in the car and headed home to pick up our kids. Gene searched the baby book as I drove and announced with genuine disappointment that no one was listed as my godparents and nothing looked suspicious or out of the ordinary. We'd hit another brick wall. When we arrived at Granny's, Gene went straight into one of the spare bedrooms with his computer, while I sat down on the sofa with my grandmother.

She was still in her bed clothes, and when I asked her about her day or if she'd eaten anything, she said that today she'd just been lollygagging and hadn't done much at all. My level of concern rose as I watched her sluggish demeanor. Before I'd left last night, I'd made her favorite ham and Swiss cheese sandwich and told her that it was in a baggie on the top shelf of the refrigerator. She told me she'd forgotten about it and when I went to get it for her, I noticed a full, untouched pot of coffee on the counter and her morning pills scattered all over the kitchen floor.

A brief glimpse from the corner of my eye, of Spanks running from the kitchen with something in his mouth, distracted me momentarily, and I yelled at Gene to catch him and check it out. He was out of the room and holding Spanky, fingers down the dog's throat before I'd finished picking up the pills and reached the living room. After a quick check of the remaining pills and determining which one Spanks may have eaten, Gene called the vet to see what he suggested. I returned my attention to Granny while we waited for the vet to call back. I gave her a new batch of her meds and watched her eat her sandwich and drink a half glass of iced tea. After the vet's call and I knew that Spanks was going to be all right, I hustled Granny into the bathroom with a fresh towel, clean dress, and undergarments. When she asked me through the door *why we had to wash the towels because weren't they clean when we used them anyway*? I knew that she was fine and my alert meter dropped back to normal.

Gene called me into the bedroom to show me something he'd found, just as I heard the shower water turn on. He had a picture up on the screen from a file named D. Paul and he asked me if I recognized the man standing on the beach with a very young Peggy. Maybe it was just because of all the secrecy surrounding it or the flat-out guilt I felt for taking my mother's files to begin with, but my face was red and I was burning up. The date read June 1976 and I was sure that I didn't know the man. Gene scrolled through at least ten more pictures of the same man and my mother romping playfully on the beach, making me wonder who was taking these photos. Could my dad have been taking them?

My father was in the Marines, but unlike Grandfather Bert, he didn't have to leave us for long periods of time on tours. He was a boot-camp drill sergeant and was home every night except when he had duty and slept over in the base barracks. From the looks of the sexual tension between this man and my mother, I was guessing no, the photographer had not been my father. Gene just stared at me. Before I could wrap my head around all of the questions that were now swarming around in it, I heard the water in the bathroom shut off.

I jumped up, closing the bedroom door behind me. Clean, properly fed and sitting comfortably in her special spot on the sofa, a pair of chocolate eyes staring up at her from her lap, she apologized for being such a mess when we'd arrived. I assured her that she was being ridiculous; that we all have those days, when Gene hollered from the other room for me. I kissed my grandmother's forehead and Brad managed to get his tongue up my nose before I could stop him. When I opened the bedroom door, Gene had his laptop shut and he was wearing an evil grin. I sat down next to him and glued my attention to his handsome face.

"What?" I asked, my eyes squinting in curiosity.

He sat up tall, and in just above a whisper he said, "You have to ask her if she knows who D. Paul is," and I felt my forehead squish into several large wrinkles. I shook my head no. He matched my no with his head bobbing an emphatic yes. I whispered even though there wasn't a chance in hell that my seventy-six-year-old grandmother could possibly have heard us.

"How am I going to explain why I know that name? And what if she tells my mother that I asked her about that name? Gene, we stole this information. My mom is going to go through the roof if she finds out we downloaded anything from her computer, especially that we stole secrets of her life. Maybe you're not afraid of my mother's wrath, but I'd like to live to see my next birthday."

We stared at each other in silence before he squeezed my hand tightly. "Cherry, I know the man in that picture is your father and before I can find out any more information about him, I need his first name."

"Well aren't you being a bit pretentious," I scoffed. We continued to stare into each other's eyes until he stood up and pulled me up to him.

"I'll go with you. Just ask nonchalantly and she won't think a thing about it," he assured me.

Right! We both knew better. Gene flipped on the television and turned it down low, while I sat on the sofa next to Granny. The news was on and knowing that my grandmother didn't give a rat's ass about the news, I asked Gene to please change it to Animal Planet. While he was searching for a granny-friendly program, I turned and looked my grandmother in the eyes. She smiled as she looked back at me.

"Granny, have you ever heard the name D. Paul, maybe a friend of my mom and dad's?" I asked.

I watched a little light bulb go off in her head and before we knew it she said, "Well dear, he wasn't a friend of your dad's, but Nora's oldest boy is named Dustin Paul. All of her kids have different names and fathers. All of my kids were raised with Nora's kids. Why do you ask? Have you heard something from Dustin?" and I felt my face turning beet-red again. Gene popped up from his chair and disappeared into the bedroom.

Day Twenty-Four

Oscar Wilde said, "Yes, death must be so beautiful...To lie in the soft brown earth with the grasses waving above one's head, and listen to silence...To have no yesterday and no tomorrow...To forget time, to forget life, to be at peace. You can help me. You can open for me the portals of death's house, for love is always with you, and love is stronger than death is."

That was what my mother penned and placed in a pocket of my father's overalls before he was laid to rest. I think about those words often and it's also what I wrote in a card to Nora's kids when she passed. Both of my brothers and my sister passed away from heart disease like my father. My doctors have told me that I am also at risk and I suppose that's the reason for all of the pills I'm taking. I try not to think about it, but when I have a bad day, sometimes it just pops up in my thoughts. Dying is just a part of the cycle of life, my mother told us kids when my dad died. I used to think my mother knew everything. I still do. She was a wise woman, yet tough as nails. My oldest brother told us kids that he caught our mother in the barn spitting nails from her mouth. It makes me laugh just thinking back on that, because although we knew he was just pulling our leg, it did present itself as a pretty funny picture in our young minds. I'd always hoped that I'd be just half the woman my mother was. I'm not sure that I am. It's a funny thought that here I am, a seventy-six-year-old woman who still misses her mom and pop. I suppose that never goes away.

Day Twenty-Five

Cherry and I made a quick trip to the grocery store today. She always leaves a pad of paper and a pen on the table next to my spot on the sofa and tells me to write down during the week the things I need from the store. Sometimes I act a fool and slip things on the list that I know will give her a chuckle. One night I was watching my program and the Turtle Man said that fresh peppermint leaves would repel rats. He showed it on the show and everything. When Cherry saw it on my list today she rolled her eyes and said, "Granny, what pray tell, do you need peppermint leaves for?"

I waited until I was strapped in and my seatbelt clicked and then looked over at her and said, "Well, lately I'm beginning to realize that there are a few big rats among us that we might have to beat off" and she erupted in laughter. Then she nodded. It must have made sense to her.

I'm beginning to realize that in life, it's all about the funny moments. If you're running low on them, you have to create some. I hope that when I make my exit from this world, people remember me for my sense of humor and gracious smiles, instead of just some old bat that they're glad to see planted under the daisies. I hope they say something along the lines of "That Dottie, she was a real different kettle of fish; a party, ready to happen." I suppose I'll never really know what they end up saying, but I'm going to keep the moments coming while I can. When we got to the check-out counter, the male cashier really took a shine to Cherry. I could tell that she was aware of it, too. Because Gene and Cherry don't wear the traditional wedding bands, the poor lad had no way of knowing she isn't available.

My granddaughter explained to me once that they both had something else to symbolize the love between them. It's my guess that it's one of those tattoos or something, not that there's anything wrong with that. It's an arrangement that suits them and makes them happy. Tony just kept up his flirting until our grocery sacks were packed, the bill paid, and we were heading to the door. He's clearly a good-looking Italian and a good five inches shorter than Cherry, with a coal-black head of hair and so thin he makes me look like an ol' heifer.

He was still looking at the exit door while I was bringing up the rear with my walker, and he yelled to Cherry, "Later today you're gonna ask yourself, should I go back to the store and give my number to that checker I met today, and you know what you're going to say?"

We both turned toward him, and Cherry gave up and said, "No, what am I going to say?" as the automatic door flew open.

"You're going to say exactly what my name spelled backward says. Have a great day!" and he went back to his register. When we were settled in the car, I asked her what the

young man meant by that. If anyone knows the strange lingo, that Cherry does. She just laughed and pulled out of our spot and headed home. She never did tell me, and maybe it's better that way. Raylan hasn't called in a few days. I'm going to have to give him a buzz tomorrow. Tea sure sounds nice right about now.

Day Twenty-Six

Today was not a good day at all. I ended up taking two naps and I still can't shake this low-energy feeling; it's like taking a sleeping pill and not understanding why I can't dance. Cherry kept asking me if I'd taken my morning pills with my coffee today and I kept telling her the same thing over and over. Yes! Raylan's daughter called while I was on nap number two and spoke to Gene. She wanted to pass a message on from Raylan that he was going to be in the hospital for a few days and left the room number and also the phone number where I could reach him. Evidently she wouldn't tell Gene the reason he was there. I tried calling, but a nurse answered and said that Raylan was out of the room having some tests done. I'm going to try again first thing in the morning.

Right now I sure wish I had my car because I'd make a trip to the store and get me some castor oil. I'm sure that's all I really need. I'd go up and visit Raylan too. Well, lights out for this old gal.

Chapter Twelve
When Pigs Fly

I did it. I finally told Gene about the letter I lifted from Granny's mailbox. With everything else going on, I'd honestly forgotten about it until last night. Gene and I had gone to bed and I was just about to drift off and *poof* I remembered that I still had it. No way I could go back to sleep with my brain in overdrive. Gene was already heavy into his first round of snoring, so I quietly left the room and opened it at the kitchen table. By candlelight and with a glass of red wine; I tried to open it carefully, so that maybe I could re-glue it; but nothing's ever that easy for me. The envelope tore so I just went ahead and ripped the sucker open. A handwritten letter was enclosed inside a Hallmark card.

Mom,

I really wish that I'd had the opportunity to speak to you while I was there, but I do hope you're feeling better. I have a question for you, the answer to which for years I honestly believed I could live without, but it has become blatantly clear to me as I've grown older, that it's no longer possible. I need to know. It's as if the fabric of my being has a hole in it that can't be patched or mended, without knowing the truth.

In 1974, just before I graduated from high school, my friends and I were on our way to a going-away party for Josh Mosey and we passed that hotel that used to be on First and Broadway. I saw Dad and two blonde-haired women leaving a room and climbing into Dad's car. All of my friends saw him too. Later that week I went to dad and asked him about it. I even told him about the two women and all he said was, "I don't do anything that your mother doesn't know about." He wouldn't explain. He gave me, his teenage son, no explanation for what clearly looked like infidelity. I was left torn between thinking that either both of you were nuts or I'd misunderstood the set of morals that both of you pounded into my head for all the years of my childhood. I could accept Dad and the whole military macho-man image, but you? I've been waiting since the day I left Santa Barbara for you to come to me and explain, but you never have. Now, I realize that you're getting older and although Erin touches base with me from time to time, I still hope that you'll reach out to me and explain. I have never said anything until recently, to any of my siblings about what I saw or the reason I left. Erin thinks it's because I'm gay and in the closet. I'm not. I am, however, still confused and still hoping that you have a logical explanation for what I saw. Please give me a call. Erin has my new number.

Love, Brock

P.S. Penny's daughter had her baby, a boy she named Hubert Henry. You'll never know how difficult it's been for me to keep my mouth shut, considering what I know, but I have zipped my lips. You might want to reach out to them.

Crap! Crap! Crap! And I try never to cuss unless it's a hundred percent justified and this is the epitome of justification. I wasn't sure about the way I was going to feel after reading Brock's letter; I only knew what he'd said wasn't at all what I'd expected. I woke Gene up. After he'd read it and picked his chin up off the table, we both started to panic a little.

"We have to get this to Granny. She has to see this for herself, so she can make things right with her son," I told him. Although his expression was blank, I could tell he agreed.

"God, I'm an evil person and a thief," I whispered. "What are we going to do?"

Gene reached for the envelope and like those cartoons where the little light bulb appears above the character's head, he calmly answered me. "Tomorrow I'll take this envelope to the store and find a card the same size. When I get home, we'll put Brock's card in the new envelope and make it look as close to his handwriting as possible," and he paused briefly to be sure we were both on the same page.

"Then you have to be sure that she opens it; you can't allow her to tuck it between the sofa cushions as she often does. When she opens it, you need to take the envelope quickly, as if you're going to throw it out but hide it somewhere so we can burn it. That way, she's got the letter but will have no idea that it had been opened. We can do this babe," and a smile swam across his face.

"Okay, let me see if I can get the old stamp off and I'll camouflage it on the new envelope tomorrow, the best I can." This had to work. "Operation Fix Cherry's Screw Up" was going down.

The next morning Gene left for the store, but not before quoting a phrase from a speech by President John F. Kennedy that he liked, "A rising tide lifts all boats," he said with a smile, as he closed the garage door behind him. I wasn't entirely sure how that was supposed to inspire me until I went to look at what he'd asked me to examine on his laptop. Dustin Jase Paul's facebook page was staring me in the face. A picture of five old boats docked at a marina was his time-line photo. Although we still weren't certain of it, Gene had decided that Dustin, Granny's acquaintance and Nora's son, was absolutely my father.

Because Granny and Nora had met in the maternity section of a hospital, that would make my mother and Dustin the same age; both fifty-nine years old. My mother and Dustin would have been either twenty-three or -four when they had the alleged affair. Gene was so sure of it, he'd completely abandoned looking into any of our former prospects. He'd found Dustin J. Paul on facebook and sent him a "friend" request, that within days was accepted.

Gene's second-to-oldest sister is a private investigator and he asked her to do some digging for us. While I was flipping through photo albums Dustin had posted, Gene returned. He sat down and we silently looked at the girls who appeared to be my age or younger. There were pictures of cute babies but no descriptions of who they were or their relation to Dustin.

"These women all look like they could be your full sisters, Cherry," he said finally.

"Ummm, I don't know about that, babe. I do know we'd better get the card ready and go to Granny's house before she sets a fire or worse," and I stood, ridding my head of all things Dustin.

Gene grabbed my hand and pulled me back down in my seat. Looking me in the eye, he spoke in just above a whisper, "Cherry, whatever you decide about all of this is completely your decision. If you want to stop right now and let it go, I'm okay with that. Please just tell me if I'm coming on too strong and it's too much. I want to help, but I don't want you to be hurt in any way because of anything I pushed you into. Talk to me, please." he smiled sweetly at me.

"I promise," I told him.

"Close your eyes." My hands were in his.

"Tell me what you see?" he asked.

"Ummm, darkness; I see nothing."

Seconds passed before he said, "That's what I imagine my life would be without you; *capiche?*"

I opened my eyes to my husband's face, inches from mine. He kissed my lips softly and I felt goose bumps up and down my arms. Yes, I truly loved this man.

Day Twenty-Seven

Memories are funny things, like kaleidoscopes. Two people can look at the same event, see the same people and places, yet each will walk away with different memories. Like fingerprints, too, I suppose. Lately my head's been plumb full of thoughts of home. Truckee was a wonderful place for a child to be raised. I often wished that Bert and I had never left, but I'm smart enough to know that our opportunities were greater here in Santa Barbara.

Our first big fight, of all things, focused on the place we both would be laid to rest. I wanted to join my parents, who were buried in Truckee, but Bert insisted that we be buried as a family here in Santa Barbara. He'd bought plots at a local cemetery for him and me, plus all of our children. His parents were buried there, he said. I was young, homesick and maybe even a little foolish, so I dug in my heels and demanded that we all be buried where he and I had met, in Truckee, beside my parents, as well as my sister and brothers. He said "when pigs fly!" We didn't speak to each other for a solid week because of it, but of course I promised him before he died, that we would all be buried together, here in Santa Barbara.

But now that he's gone, how would he ever know? I'm seriously thinking about being shipped to Truckee when I leave this earth. I haven't been back since my mother died. When my siblings passed, I attended each funeral but didn't get to attend the burials. Their immediate families escorted their bodies back to Truckee, but I didn't get to go. I regret that now. I know having us all in the same cemetery would please my parents.

Maybe I should get hold of that lawyer Nora went to see and ask his opinion. Yes, I believe I'll do that. Cherry is taking me up to the hospital to see Raylan tomorrow. I'm going to get my bath early and spritz myself with some perfume and do what Gene often tells Cherry he's going to do. I'm going to get my swagger on.

Day Twenty-Eight

Today dragged long, but turned out to be a pretty good day. I got myself all dolled up for Raylan and Gene stayed at my house with the dogs, while Cherry drove me to the hospital. When we finally found his room, Cherry waited outside in the hallway while I went in to see Raylan.

I was taken aback when I first laid eyes on him; he didn't look at all that well, but his eyes lit up like a string of holiday lights when he saw me. "Well if you don't look prettier than a gob of butter melting on a tall stack of flapjacks," he howled, but it was sure good to see him. I sat with him and asked how he was feeling.

He said, "Everything hurts and what doesn't ache, isn't working." It seems that Raylan had some down-south man issues and I could tell he was a tad embarrassed about sharing it with me. I did my best to lift his spirits and when I learned that his couple of days at the hospital had snowballed into another week, I excused myself and stepped out into the hall and asked Cherry to run home and fetch me a few things. Maybe it was me; oh whose leg am I pulling? I'm sure it was me but Cherry kept repeating the things that I'd asked for all wrong, so before we both got any more frustrated, she pulled out a pen and paper from her purse and wrote everything down. Once I was satisfied that she had it all straight, she high-tailed it for the house, but not before making me promise to stay put. I agreed, but honestly, how far did the child think me and my walker were going to get?

What happened next, no one could have foreseen. When I went back in and sat down next to Raylan, he gazed out the window at the sky, then reached for my hand, which I gladly gave to him, and said, "Rose, when they let me out of here, I'm thinking about taking a little trip and I'd be so honored if you'd *consider accompanying me," and his tired-looking eyes settled on mine. I wasn't yet sure if he was just flirting with this old gal, but the more I stared into his eyes, the more I realized he was as serious as a mosquito looking for its next meal. Before I could come up with something intelligent to say, he continued. "I'd like to visit Butchart Gardens; I've always said that I was going to visit that place and then something always popped up, so I never made it. I'm eighty-three years old and I think it's time that I go see what some people have called the prettiest garden ever."*

Well if that didn't put pepper in my gumbo! The only Butchart Gardens I know is located in Brentwood Bay, British Columbia, Canada, near Victoria. A vision of Cherry's face flashed in my mind. She doesn't even want me to shower when she's not there. She's not going to be at all pleased about a road trip. Looking into his fragile and pale face snapped me back from my silly thoughts, but the look in his sunken eyes told me that he was still as serious as a hungry fox in a chicken coop. That reality may have stunned me for a brief moment but then something screamed inside me to say yes. I told him when he got well enough to travel, I'd love to make the trip with him, even suggesting that maybe we could swing by my hometown on our way back. He just smiled at me and squeezed my hand tightly.

Just about then, Cherry showed up with the items I'd requested and together, we got busy fixing up Raylan's room properly. We hung my favorite pictures of an ocean before sunset and one of beautiful butterflies taking off from a patch of brightly colored wildflowers. Next we spread my favorite cozy blanket from my sofa, dog hairs and all, on the bottom of his bed. My two best feather pillows were put in place and a dish of assorted candies on his bedside table. As we were finishing up, his daughter arrived and we introduced ourselves. Raylan was grinning from ear-to-ear. When his lunch arrived, we said our goodbyes and Raylan made me promise to call him later this evening. I kissed his forehead and we headed home. Gene had made us spaghetti and used more onion than this old gal can handle, but it was yummy. The lad can cook. Cherry gave me something for my heartburn and then they left at nine o'clock.

I called Raylan and he sounded relaxed. I asked him if he'd do me a favor and ask his daughter to fetch him a bottle of castor oil and I'd repay her when I saw her next time. He said he'd be more than happy to, and thanked me again for my visit. I felt good when I told him goodnight. Yes, it was a good day. I think I'll have a cup of vanilla Sleepy-Time tea.

Day Twenty-Nine

Today I have truly been discombobulated, like a cork bobbing in the ocean. Cherry handed me a letter when she came in from fetching the mail and surprised me with a letter from Brock. After handing it to me, she disappeared into the kitchen briefly, only to reappear and snatched the envelope from my lap without giving me a moment's notice. She seemed as nervous as a cat in a room full of rockers. I think something fishy is going on there but I haven't been able to place my finger on it yet. The card Brock sent is beautiful, a vase of daisies with the words, "I hope you are feeling better, Mom," but the letter inside caught me a tad off guard. It seems he saw something that happened way back in

1974, that's troubled him all these years and I had no idea he knew anything about this particular incident. What upsets me most is that I'm just now finding out that Bert was aware of his son's knowledge and never thought to share it with me. I feel a bit betrayed right now, like a trapped mouse eating its last bit of cheese. I haven't thought about any of this in a coon's age and I'm not sure if it would be better to call my son or just pen him a letter. I believe I'll fix myself a cup of tea and sleep on it.

Day Thirty

After thinking about nothing else all morning, I decided to ask Cherry what she would do if she were in my predicament. I'm sure as a cat with climbing gear that she's going to catch wind of it anyway, so I thought maybe with her help, I'd be sure to make the right decision on telling Brock the truth about what he saw. She was more than happy to listen and at the end, I believe she offered me some sound advice. She suggested that I think back to the time I was living at home, before I left and got married, and picture the way I would've felt if I'd witnessed the same scenario. Well, her advice made things clear as a bell to me and I picked up the phone and gave my son a call. We talked for a good hour or so and I believe that things will now be much better between us. That's all I really hoped for.

Later, Gene showed Cherry and me a video on his traveling computer, of a grown man doing some fancy dancing called Gangnam Style. We all had a pretty good laugh over the video before sitting down for a tasty supper of tomato soup plus grilled ham-and-cheese sandwiches. I called Raylan after we ate and he seemed to be frustrated that he hadn't yet been given a date when he could check out and go home. He did say that he had a bottle of castor oil waiting for me. I think I'd like to go see him tomorrow if Cherry will drive me. Tomorrow is our usual house-spiffing-up day, so we'll see.

Chapter Thirteen
"Slipperier Than a Greased Pig at a Hog-Tying Competition"

I was running late, Gene and the dogs all standing at the back door waiting patiently for me to finish gathering up my things. With laptop, purse and bag of dinner fixings in hand, Gene opened the door and yelled, "Let it rip, tater chips," and the dogs and I shuffled through the garage to the car. My morning had been moving pretty smoothly until thirty minutes before we were planning to leave. My sister called, saying she had some information she wanted to share; something she'd learned during her lunch date with our mother. After a whole week; she'd finally decided that it was bothering her enough that she'd call and tell me about it. Then, making me promise a half dozen times I would not tell anyone the source of the information, she finally spilled the beans.

My mother had convinced her sisters Reese and Erin, to give Granny's house to my brother Michael when she finally passed. Not only did I find that grossly premature but also a little morbid; luckily for me, Granny and Heather did, too. My sister said that Peggy had asked Uncle Brock about it and although he hadn't agreed, he said he didn't care. She also said that, per the copy of the will my mother had prepared prior to her father's passing, it listed the house and its contents to be fairly divided between the five children. My mother figured that Granny's house was too old and too small for any of her siblings' liking, and so she'd decided my brother Michael needed it more than any other family member.

My brother, although I love him dearly, is a screw-up. He's never married, has three children with two different mothers, which is fine. *"Shit happens!"* The kicker for me is that he's never lived in the same place for more than six months. He's just fine crashing at someone's house until Mr. Generous becomes tired of it and kicks him out. He's thirty-seven years old, for Pete's sake. He takes his kids to my mother's house for his overnight visitations Friday, Saturday, and Sunday, twice a month, because the court demands that he have a stable environment for them. After talking it through with my sister, it's our guess that this arrangement is wearing on my mother's nerves. Her solution? Give him Granny's house. She's a peach, my mother; pit, fuzz, and all. I honestly didn't care what they did as long as it all went down after my grandmother passed. Hearing about this plan now made more sense regarding my mother's relentless efforts to put Granny in a nursing home. She wasn't dying fast enough so let's ship her off to an old folks' home. Let's put Old Ironsides in dry dock.

When we arrived at my grandmother's, I ran across the street to the mailbox, realizing that I'd forgotten to check it yesterday and slipped the card from Brock in the middle of the stack. I wouldn't be able to look her in the eye when I gave it to her; I was sure guilt would be spread all over my face like cookie crumbs after a cookie raid. Luckily, Gene and I had worked out a plan to help solve my guilt problem; well, mask it anyway, and we executed it perfectly. I handed Granny the mail and Gene stayed in the living room as he usually did, messing around on his computer, while I slipped into the kitchen. He was to clear his throat twice when she had the card out of the envelope and on her lap and then I would scurry in and whisk away the tainted evidence, stuffing it in my pocket to be burned later. That part went down perfectly, but after she read the letter, she placed it back into the card and did exactly what she'd done with the book she received from Raylan. She tucked it between the sofa cushions without so much as a word, as if it had never happened. It was an epic failure for Gene and me. We were hoping to get some answers; some juicy dirt, and tingly tidbits. We got *nada*.

After lunch, Granny told me about Aunt Cricket's conversation with her when she'd come to visit last week. My aunt had sent Gene and me out to buy some ice cream for all of us, even though I'd shown her a full half gallon of Neapolitan in Granny's freezer. She was an accessory to my mother's little scheme; she'd been sent to do the dirty work, which was a typical Sergeant Peggy ploy. Of course my mother wouldn't want to get her hands dirty; that's not the way she rolled.

Day Thirty-One

On my first cup of coffee, the phone rang. I answered and the conversation went like this:

Me: Hello

Caller: Knock, Knock!

Me: Who's there?

Caller: Lettuce.

Me: Lettuce who?

Caller: Lettuce in.

Me: Okay, I'm going to set the phone down so I can get up and answer it.

Me: Hello.

Caller: Knock, Knock!

Me: Who's there?

Caller: Honey bee.

Me: Honey bee who?

Caller: Honey bee a dear and get me a soda.

Me: Sorry, I only have iced tea.

Click! I never did find out who it was that called. I'm sure it was a child, just not sure whose youngster.

Then I took my bath. Twice. I know exactly what happened now, anyway. I have a sitting chair in my tub and I stand up, soap up, and then sit back down. The spray contraption is wonderful because it's long enough that I can just remain sitting and spray all the soap right off my wrinkled skin like a snake, shedding.

I did, however, forget to stand and rinse my private parts, so while I was drying off, I noticed my undercarriage was slipperier than a greased pig at a hog-tying competition. I got back in the tub and heard a little tap on the door, "Granny, you okay in there?" When she heard the water go back on, she must have thought her grandmother was plumb up a pole.

Raylan's daughter called while I was in the powder room and told Cherry that he'd been moved to another room and he wasn't allowed to have anything that wasn't sterile or doctor-approved in his new room. She asked if she could drop off the things we'd brought to decorate his room and Cherry agreed. When she arrived, she said that for the next several days, only immediate family would be allowed to visit and that really

saddened me. I fished a card from my desk and filled it out before

she left and asked her if she'd pass it on to Raylan. She said she'd

be happy to, and let's hope that she doesn't go opening it like some

of my kinfolk do. My castor oil was in the box full of items and

guess which person didn't catch wind of it? My granddaughter!

Yes, today was a tad crazy, but not a bad day by any means. I

asked Cherry if Brad Pitt could sleep over tonight and she allowed

the little man to stay. It's getting late and I believe he and I will

get us a cup of tea before turning out the lights and turning in.

Day Thirty-Two

I had a bit of a mishap with the bottle of castor oil today. I

was worried that Cherry would find it, so after two tablespoons of

my liquid gold, I hid the bottle under my mattress, thinking it was

tucked away safe and sound. I must not have tightened the cap

securely enough because after my coffee, I realized that Brad was

missing and I found him licking up a puddle of castor oil from my

bedroom floor. When I checked the bottle, nearly half the oil was gone. I had two spoonfuls and Brad had lapped up half a bottle. I quickly chose another hiding place but I was sure worried sick about Brad. He seemed fine when the kids arrived and when Gene gave him his breakfast, he wolfed it down like he usually does. Just when I was breathing easy and thought that everything was hunky dory, Mr. Pitt had himself an accident by the back door. Then Gene said he threw up his breakfast outside and sat hunched up relieving himself for several minutes. The kids were a little suspicious at first, but when I swore to them I was sure that I'd not dropped any of my morning pills, they shrugged it off to a mild tummy ache. That was a close call. I was two shakes away from 'fessin' up about the castor oil caper. By lunch, Brad was better than snuff and not half dusty.

I asked Cherry if she'd mind calling the hospital to check up on Raylan and she happily made the call. While she was busy on the phone, Gene left to run an errand and I decided to pull out the book Rootabagas Stories *and allow my mind to escape the worries I'd been feeling. I needed to travel to a place that was just plumb full of fun. After an update on Raylan, Cherry disappeared into the kitchen to do laundry and start the casserole for dinner. She gave me a silly grin when she saw my book but she didn't spill a word about it. After dinner we watched "Dirty Harry." If I had a nickel for every time I'd heard Bert recite Harry Callahan's famous movie dialogue, the kids and I would be sitting on some warm tropical beach holding one of those fancy-pants drinks with a paper umbrella on it. Gene stopped the movie and muted the sound so I could take the floor. I cleared my throat and with all eyes on me, I proceeded.*

"I know what you're thinking. Did he fire six shots or only five? Well, to tell you the truth, in all this excitement I kind of lost track. But because this is a .44 Magnum, the most powerful handgun in the world and would blow your head clean off, you've got to ask yourself one question: Do I feel lucky? Well, do ya, punk?" I took a bow and the kids gave me a round of applause for my perfect performance. I miss you, Bert!

Day Thirty-Three

Cherry dropped Gene and the dogs off this morning and left to run some errands. While I was sipping my coffee, I had a little epiphany. I was watching Gene on the floor, playing with the dogs, as they squirmed and squeaked, yanking at his pants legs with excitement and it dawned on me who he looks like. I've always thought he reminded me of someone. Lo and behold if he doesn't look like David Cassidy from "The Partridge Family." His brown shag-like haircut and baby face screams David Cassidy. I know a thing or two about that bubble gum pop star that had me enduring years of the song "I think I love you," screamed at the top of their lungs from at least three of my teenage girls' pie holes. Oh they had some huge crushes on that David; Bobby Sherman, too. Reese had it for him the worst. I caught her kissing the poster hanging above her bed one night. Wow, I'm not sure what made me remember that after all these years.

Penny was the challenge of my four girls. She was into anything rock and roll; music, clothes, and attitude. She was and always has been a bit of a loner and a person of few words. When she did say something, everyone stopped and listened. I'd always felt as if Penny was Bert's favorite, although he'd never come out and said it. They both just seemed to understand each other on a level the rest of us could not comprehend. Maybe it had something to do with military mannerisms. Penny followed in Bert's footsteps and was a Marine for four years before moving to Utah. Years after all the kids had left home and Bert and I moved back into the first house we'd bought, we got to looking through some old photos together. I noticed that Penny was always standing off to the side, like an onlooker rather than a family member. Bert mentioned with a serious face that she was a thinker and an observer, like the statue of Rodin. I'm not sure about his analogy but she and I aren't any closer than we were when she was a child.

I always felt she loved me, just not really needed me like the others did. She fended for herself and was quite independent. Her twin brother, on the other hand, was quite the opposite. If I sat down and had a free lap, that boy's radar went off and he'd be using his climbing gear to get to me. He used to grab both sides of my face with his chubby little hands and with his hot breath inches from my face, say, "Mama, this is wealy impo'tant," even if it wasn't. It always was to him. I miss that little boy. Some days I miss them all.

Lately and with a special few, I sometimes think, "And for you I have stretch marks and a droopy butt." Before Cherry returned, I asked Gene if he'd ever been told he favored David Cassidy and he smiled, his lips tightening into a thin line before he spoke.

"Yes, and I was told by Cherry's mom when we first met that it was the only reason she could find for liking me." I chuckled to myself because that sounded exactly like something my holier-than-thou daughter would say. Well, that castor oil really seems to be helping, but I'm still a tad worn out from the long day. I believe its tea time and then lights out for me.

Day Thirty-Four

At eleven-thirty this evening, while I was watching my program, the telephone rang. Nothing good comes from a call that late at night, and when I answered, it was Nancy, Raylan's daughter. She said that Raylan asked to see me and that if I was going to visit, it had to be now. I hung up and dialed 4-1-1 and asked a cab to come fetch me. I didn't make it, but I did get to sit with him alone and hold his hand to say good bye. It's now four in the morning and I can't sleep. I've lost so many people over my lifetime and I keep thinking that it's going to get easier somehow, but it never does. It's like taking castor oil; hold your nose and swallow! I'll miss my friend.

"Love's Secret"
Never seek to tell thy love,
Love that never told can be;
For the gentle wind does move
Silently, invisibly.

I told my love, I told my love,
I told her all my heart;
Trembling, cold, in ghastly fears,
Ah! She did depart!

Soon as she was gone from me,
A traveler came by,
Silently, invisibly
He took her with a sigh.
~William Blake ~

This poem was inside an envelope in the bedside table of my dear

friend Raylan. It was addressed to Rose, and the note read:

Though it looks as though we won't get the chance to make

our trip, I know we will meet again. I feel so very fortunate to

have met you, and I am a lucky man to have been in the company

of such a beautiful Rose.

All my love, Raylan

Chapter Fourteen
"Insemination in a Motel Room"

My mother and I have struggled lately to have a civil conversation between us and by lately, I mean since the bizarre family meeting to which Gene and I were summoned. She and I were now clearly on opposite sides of the fence and I'd caught myself being sharp and slightly distasteful with her. Regurgitating her words and demeanor from that meeting felt similar to a nauseating bout of stomach flu. As if that ordeal wasn't enough, there were all of the unspoken questions I wanted to ask but managed to refrain from spurting out; the questions and accusations I felt she had coming, the family scandal she'd created and the uncertainty of what was going to happen when the dust finally settled.

Back when all of us kids were teenagers and still living at home, whenever a parental problem arose, my big bad drill-sergeant father would bail, after making the rules or punishments by stating, "I have no dog in this fight" and he'd leave the room, heading for safer ground.

Now, however, I very much felt like he did have a dog in this fight, and because I had more questions than answers, he was the biggest reason I hadn't already exploded like Mount Etna. He didn't have to ask for it, but I felt he deserved my respect. My mother, on the other hand, never sought sympathy or requested anyone's approval. She'd always felt entitled; she was owed our loyalty and respect. Up until the day I left home, and even recently, I'd always followed her rules and played the game accordingly. Some ugly game changes had now surfaced from Peg's big pot of potash.

My mother was now the enemy and number one on my personal black list. I could feel, deep within my bones, a dark storm brewing and lightning striking in the near future almost like a fork tine stuck in an electrical outlet. Peggy's fairytale world was quickly coming to an end. I wasn't sure when the sky was going to fall, only that it was going to fall on Miss Chicken Little.

When we arrived at Granny's and I saw the frail, fragile little woman sitting in her favorite place there on the sofa, I managed to shove all things Peggy down as far as I possibly could into the cellar of my mind. Granny seemed to pull up from me a protective, motherly persona I once believed was only there for my canine kids. Today she was sitting in her bed clothes, her hair down and flowing to her waist. Gene and I usually weren't privy to seeing her hair in anything but a loose bun. In her lap was a hairbrush and the card from Brock that she'd received in the mail. I sat down next to her while Gene disappeared with the dogs, into the backyard. I reached for the hairbrush and she smiled, turning herself so that I could brush her hair. Her long gray locks were silky soft.

"How are you feeling today, Granny?" I asked.

"How are you feeling, Cherry?" she chirped.

"Granny, you're deflecting. I'd really like to know how you're feeling today," I said firmly.

"I'm fine, dear, but I'd like to get something off my chest that's bothering me and if you wouldn't mind, I'd like to share it with you and maybe ask your advice about something too."

I continued brushing her hair before twisting it up into a loose bun and pulling a scrunchy from my hair, I wrapped it up and gave her shoulders a little squeeze with my hands when I was finished. My pause was deliberate. Of course I was dying to know what was bothering her; I just didn't want to sound overly exuberant about it. She turned and looked me in the eye, still waiting for an answer to her question. "Oh good gravy Granny, you know that you can talk to me about anything, I'm all ears" and I gave her a little wink. She smiled, both dimples showing in her rosy cheeks. "Does this have something to do with Uncle Brock's card?" I asked.

She grabbed the brush that was sitting between us, then turning, placed it on the table before turning her attention to me. Opening the card, she took the handwritten letter out and handed it to me. I accepted it, my eyes still watching her face, and a rush of what I'm sure was probably guilt, filled my face, raising my temperature a degree or two. She didn't ask me to read it, a clear indication that she knew I already had. Epic failure, Cherry! What she said next was far better than anything Gene or I could ever have imagined. We hit the family-smut lottery! She began at the beginning and I didn't interrupt her. Before Uncle Brock saw his father and the two women at the hotel, a great deal had happened first, to get them there.

In 1973, Granny's dear friend Nora introduced her cousin Vivian and her partner Frieda to my grandparents. The cousin and her partner were purchasing a house in Santa Barbara, moving there from Texas, and staying with Nora and family for a six-week stretch until they were able to move into their new home. Vivian and Frieda were lesbians during a time when most folks weren't all that accepting, my grandmother explained, and so they kept much about their relationship at a low volume.

Eventually Granny grew close to Nora's cousin and the four played cards together every Friday night and watched movies often, too. Once Vivian and Frieda were settled in their new home, they were eager to expand their family and began checking into the adoption process. Because society wasn't as open-minded as it is today, many doors were slammed shut in their faces and they began exploring other options. The thing I didn't know and I'm positive Uncle Brock didn't know, was that Nora was a fertility-nurse practitioner. She worked for a doctor who specialized in blessing families that seemed doomed never to conceive on their own. Eventually all four women got to talking and before long, my grandfather was enlisted to donate his sperm to help Nora's childless cousin and her partner. Granny explained that at first Bert refused, because he thought the whole thing was just unnatural, like messing with Mother Nature, but after some desperate convincing and a well-orchestrated ambush by all four women, he was finally talked into it. He requested only that his name stay off the birth certificate. Everyone agreed. Because neither woman's insurance would cover the procedure, Nora decided it would be best to do it at a hotel, off the radar screen.

Brock didn't know Nora was in the hotel room that day. Granny said she'd prepared the bathroom for Bert, just like the one at the fertility hospital and when he was finished filling the specimen jar with his semen, he went across the street to a bar and waited for Nora to inseminate both women. She also said that Nora was there on her lunch hour and running late, so Bert agreed to drive Vivian and Frieda to their house when they were finished with the procedure. Granny said it was just like Christmas, waiting to hear if either of the women became pregnant. They both conceived and delivered three days apart. A little boy named Michael and a little girl, Hazel, came into this world. My grandmother said it was the best gift she and Bert had ever given anyone and until Nora passed, the cousin sent her pictures of the boy and girl, religiously. Granny asked me if she should pen a note to Brock, call him, or keep it under her hat. I encouraged her to call him.

Day Thirty-Five

Holy mother-of-pearl, I really went and did it this time. When the kids arrived this morning, I was still asleep in my bed and was awakened when Cherry threw the covers off me and jumped into the bed, ready to perform C.P.R. To say that I was startled is an understatement and we both just froze, staring at each other like a couple of surprised raccoons on a late-night trash-bin foray. Gene finally calmed her down after she learned about my little trip to the hospital last night, and that girl flew off the handle big time, like some wound-up toy popping all its springs

and whistles. All I said was that I took a cab and went to see

Raylan but she was huffing and puffing around the house so fast, I

had trouble keeping up. She was throwing both of her hands in the

air and her face was as red as a fire engine. If Peggy were to

catch wind of my infraction, she'd have me packed up and shipped

off to some old folks' home so fast, my head would spin on the way

out the door. Again, Gene was able to calm Cherry down. At one

point she was so angry at both of us, she just walked in circles and

blew raspberries at Gene and me like some little kid sassing her

parent. I'm still not clear on what poor Gene did.

I really wanted a cup of coffee, but I didn't dare ask. She

needed to get it all out of her system and Gene, the dogs, and I sat

very still on the sofa and let her rant and rave until she came to a

halt, like an unwound top. By lunch time, she wasn't talking to me

but she wasn't yelling anymore either. By supper time she seemed

to have calmed down and sent Gene out to pick up pizza. I'm not

really fond of pizza, but she knew that and this was payback. After

we ate, I finally piped up and asked her if she'd mind helping me send an arrangement of flowers to Raylan's family and she gladly agreed to help. I believe the girl has had a lot on her plate lately and I probably haven't been much help to her in that department. She sort of apologized for getting so upset today, but in the same breath chastised me for not calling her first. She told me she loved me and that I'd scared the livin' daylights out of her and that I could call her anytime I needed anything and she'd be there, no matter what time of day or night. She rattled on like a squeaky locomotive on its last puff of steam. I explained I wasn't thinking straight, and we hugged so tight it could have brought tears to a pair of glass eyes. I love that child

Chapter Fifteen
"Crayola Crayons and Orange Creamsicles"

The phone rang at six-fifteen a.m. and Gene reached over me and Spanks to answer it. I'd been up late last night filling store orders and hadn't made it to bed until after three o'clock.

I heard, "Yep. All-righty then, I'll tell her" before my husband rolled back over me, his hairy armpit brushing across my face as he replaced the phone in its cradle.

"Who was that?" I asked, squinting at the clock.

"It was your mother; she wants to see you at her house this morning at nine," and he rolled out of bed and headed for the bathroom, but not before giving me a sympathetic glance my way.

"What the flip!" I groaned and lay there patiently waiting for his return. She had to have said something more. Didn't she give even a hint what she wanted to see me about? Why should I even go? Who does she think she is? Do I drop everything and answer to her beck and call?

I heard the toilet flush and Gene yelled, "Let's go, guys," as he briskly clapped his hands. No one moved. It was like this every morning. Our secret weapon was racing downstairs and opening the refrigerator door while singing loudly, "Mmm...good!" and "Oh...who's hungry?" Only then would little butts start moving. The promise of a hotdog tidbit, which is a little ironic in a house full of wieners, was the only morning motivation with which we'd had any success. I followed the herd of dogs down the stairs and plopped down in a kitchen chair to continue my line of questioning regarding my mother's call. Gene placed a cup of coffee in front of me and headed toward the back door to release the hounds into the yard. Grabbing his cup, he sat across the table from me and smirked but said nothing.

"So," I said, "did my mom say why she wanted to see me, or why she found it necessary to call at the crack of dawn?"

He pulled his cup to his lips, gently shaking his head no.

"Great!" I scoffed. We continued to sit quietly for several minutes before Gene finally let out a giggle. With his eyes twinkling and his handsome face lit up like Main Street at holiday time, he said, "I believe this appointment with your mother calls for some appropriate attire," and I squinted curiously at him while taking a quick sip from my cup.

"What's appropriate attire?" I questioned. He chuckled and stood up to open the back door for the now-whining wieners.

"Well I figure she wants to talk to you about one of two things," and he paused, waiting for all of the growling and yapping to simmer down. "A, she's found a facility to ship Granny off to, or B, she's going to 'fess up and tell you about your real dad before her mother is able to beat her to the punch. Either way, I believe the meeting will be dark; therefore, black funeral clothing is in order" and he winked at me for effect.

"You, Eugene Thomas Cones, are a freak! Where do you get this Shinola?" and I laughed.

"It's a gift," he answered and we headed for the stairs to shower and dress. Leaving the dogs at home, we headed for my mother's house but first stopped for a breakfast burrito at the urging of Gene's rumbling stomach. Although I wasn't looking forward to an encounter with Peggy, my curiosity had been piqued. Gene's sister, the private investigator, had called us with an address she'd found for Dustin J. Paul, but because of the recent loss of Granny's friend Raylan, *Dustin* had been stored farther back in our mental Rolodex. Lately, my grandmother had been a bit more emotionally needy than usual, but overall, I thought she'd been holding up pretty well. Raylan's funeral was scheduled to be held in his hometown of San Diego, making my grandmother's attendance unlikely and I knew that bit of news was disappointing for her. She's requested, on several nights, that one of the dogs be allowed to stay with her for company and it seemed to be helping take her mind off her melancholy.

When we pulled up to Peggy's house, we could see her standing on the front porch, her arms crossed, obviously waiting on us DINKs. It was seven minutes after nine and her posture was clearly announcing her displeasure with our tardiness.

I threw a look at Gene and we exited the car, but he just shrugged his shoulders before whispering, "She said around nine."

We followed her inside to the living room, where two cups of hot tea were waiting for us, sitting on the coffee table. As Gene and I sat down, the house phone rang and my mother disappeared into the kitchen to answer it. When she returned, the room's cold ambiance felt as if she wanted to tell us the reason why she'd summoned us and then send us on our way. I'm not a tea drinker, something my mother knew; but I thanked her anyway and we sat waiting for the bomb to plummet from the sky and explode, shooting shrapnel all over the place.

Within minutes it was clear that she'd only wanted me to come and Gene's *accompaniment* wasn't at all what she'd anticipated. That was confusing to us for about a minute anyway. The floodgates opened and the worst-case scenario came rushing out at us. The relationship between my mother and me was about to change permanently and would never again be the same; like filling a picture in a coloring book and knowing it could never be uncolored.

"How has your grandmother been?" she finally asked. I felt my fists clench tightly as I used them to push myself back on the seat of the sofa.

"Well she's been great, Mom, and you'd know that yourself if you ever called or stopped by," and I purposely looked bug-eyed at her. I watched as she sat down in the chair across the small room from us, her arms crossed tightly, her lips pursed in obvious annoyance. She looked at the floor rather than at us, almost as if she were reaching within herself for the courage to speak the words she had prepared to issue on our behalf.

"I trusted that you were taking good care of her Cherise, and because of some important decisions I've been forced to make on her behalf, it was easier to accomplish them while not seeing her, so that my emotions wouldn't cloud my judgment" and she looked up at me as if she despised me for making her explain herself. Her eyes darted from mine to Gene's. "Gene, would you wait in the other room so I can speak to my daughter privately?"

I could feel my husband's eyes on me but I didn't break my stare from Peggy to look at him.

"Why, Mom?" I demanded.

Gene stood up and bent down to kiss the top of my head before whispering to me, "I'll be in the other room if you need me." A sudden anger welled up in me like Etna ready to spew its fiery contents. My eyes fixed on my mother, watching her Adam's apple move as she swallowed hard.

When Gene left the room, my mother and I stared at each other for what seemed to be forever before she acknowledged me. "It seems that you and I have some things about which we need to have a mature conversation, Cherise," and disbelief squeezed my chest. The reality of the circumstances was evident in her eyes and tears began running down her face.

"Why am I really here, Mom?" I demanded again; repulsed at her assumption that she could distract me with tears, from the real reason we were having this conversation, to begin with. "If this is about my father, Dustin, I already know all about him. I know that you named me after Granny's mother to buy her silence, so you can call the dogs off her now Mom. I know that's the reason you want to shuffle her off to a nursing home, so that Michael can have her house to bring his kids to for visitation. I know everything Mom, and so does Gene. Can he come back into the room now?" She sat frozen; appearing to be shocked by my words. Maybe she'd rehearsed it. I felt a tear suddenly leave my left eye when I finally blinked.

"So you've told your brother about all of this, too?" she asked. Guilt riddled over her face like a child's quandary after being caught raiding the cookie jar.

"No, I haven't told anyone anything" I started wiping my face with the sleeve of my shirt. "Why would I go and do that?"

"Well, I'm sorry you had to hear about this from someone other than me. It wasn't something I was proud of and for both yours and Michael's sake, I did what I thought was best for the both of you." Her expression was sincere as I watched her crumble in shame. I contemplated letting her off the hook, on which she'd so clearly hung herself, until something inside me clicked. I stared at her for a long moment before hearing my own nervous chuckle.

"Wait. Did you just admit to me that Dustin is both mine and Michael's biological father?" Her face went white and a glaze of disbelief settled in her eyes.

Day Thirty-Six

I wrote on my grocery list today that I wanted a brand new box of Crayola Crayons and a package of orange Creamsicles, hoping to make Cherry smile. They had announced before leaving last night that they'd drop by early to bring the dogs before making a quick trip to the grocery store. Things between Cherry and me seemed right as rain and her trusting me to care for the grand-babies was her subtle way of telling me so. As soon as the door shut behind the kids, Jennifer trotted over, dropping her squeaky toy at my feet; her favorite stuffed chipmunk-looking thing that she keeps as soggy as milk-sopped bread. She'll sit at my feet, holding the darn thing in her mouth until I reach for it and toss it across the room. She'd do that all day if someone didn't take it away and hide it.

Ryan is the tail-chasing clown of the brood, and also the first to jump in my lap if he senses that I'm upset in the slightest way. Ryan to the rescue! I never say so out loud, but Ryan is my favorite.

Brad's the food thief. He'll snatch something from another's mouth if he can get away with it, and he loves to be perched in my lap too.

Princess is the shy one but that girl is a digger. She's got my backyard looking like a giant slab of Swiss cheese and I believe that secretly she's secretly making string cheese.

Angelina is the attention whore as Gene so lovingly calls her. She's the first one in the door and the last one out; always looking for an extra pat on the head when she can score one.

Spanks is the lazy lover boy. He wants everyone to love on him but always at his convenience. He has a bed in the dining room, where he's a permanent fixture. I think he tries to stay out from under everyone's feet and likes a neutral place to daydream. That boy is definitely partial to Cherry. I think he'd walk over hot coals to get to her first when the kids return from an outing.

I sure have been fortunate to have them be part of my life. My mother used to say that dogs are the most calming creatures a human could ever have and I agree. Time for tea and I'm hankering for something to satisfy my sweet tooth too. Mother always said that *"craving is like caving in"* and that we needed to pinch it in the bud.

Day Thirty-Seven

Edgar Watson Howe said, "The man who can keep a secret may be wise, but he is not half as wise as the man with no secrets to keep."

The kids showed up later than usual this morning and Cherry was wound tighter than the skin on a grape. I was pretty darn proud that I was dressed before they got here but I'm not sure either of them noticed. Cherry sat down next to me on the sofa and started rattling off questions about things she needed to know if I had known. I assured her that I'd told her everything I knew, and it was only that Peggy was seeing a fella behind her husband's back and she was going to have a child as a result of that relationship. I had no idea who the fella was and honestly I never had the slightest hankering to know. My daughter asked me to cover for her and although I knew that she was doing something she shouldn't have been, she'd explained that she'd felt unappreciated and was thinking about leaving her marriage. I assumed that she and Harry were just going through a rough patch until I showed up early at her house one day and saw a man leaving through the back door. I didn't see who it was and Peggy never told me. That's when I found out that she was pregnant and that it wasn't her husband's child. She begged me never to speak of it and promised me she was going to get her emotional house in order for the children. I never did say a word. I've never been one to judge people, at least I sure try not to judge, lest I be judged.

Both Gene and Cherry seemed upset about something for the rest of the day and it was all that I could do not to just come right out and ask what was troubling them. I'm guessing that Peggy had something to do with it all and it usually meant a need-to-know situation when it came to me. Maybe they'll be more forthcoming about it tomorrow. They did leave Jennifer here with me for the evening; she and I just shared a slice of apple pie. I suppose I'd better turn in now; it seems I have a doctor's appointment in the morning. Yippee!!!!

Day Thirty-Eight

My mother always said that promptness shows respect. Nora used to say that she liked to be fashionably late, and I'll have to admit that I never really understood that part of her. She'd tell me that she purposely arrived late to a function so that her entrance was the most anticipated. It's just plain aggravating, if you ask me. So is sitting in a doctor's cold examination room wearing nothing but a thin paper gown and the doctor is more than forty-five minutes late. Makes you wonder why the person scheduling the appointments still has a job. Then when the doc shows up, he says I need to have a stress test. His words just dilled my pickle. I wouldn't have been stressed if he'd just shown up on time.

The kids took me out to dinner tonight and then we drove around looking for an address they never did seem to find. We went right past Nora's old house but I didn't say anything about it. I thought it might make me cry.

Well Sleepy Time tea, here I come. The kids will be here early tomorrow. Cherry announced that she has a surprise for me.

The *Second Diary* 178

I'm as curious as a Cheshire cat and a tad bit excited too, like a child on Christmas morning, hoping it's the present I've always wanted.

Day Thirty-Nine

Well today I was both surprised and flabbergasted, all at the same time. Just when you think at seventy-six you've seen and heard it all, holy mackerel, something comes along and literally unzips your zipper. Cherry and Gene sat me down first thing this morning with donuts and coffee; then they shared some news they'd stumbled upon. It seems they did find Cherry's biological daddy and during their top-secret investigation, they also learned that this man was also her brother Michael's father, too. I didn't see that coming but what she said next, well, that was a revelation that still has me a little numb. She said that her father, Peg's secret lover, was my best friend's oldest boy, Dustin.

I thought my dentures were going to fall out when she said his name. I couldn't do a darn thing but start bellowing because I so badly wanted to pick up the phone and tell my best friend that we were grandparents together. The wool had been pulled over both our eyes. Then I became angrier than a bull being poked with a sword. I hadn't spoken to Melanie Margarita since the day of my birthday party but I had half a mind to pick up the phone, dial her number, and chew her out big time. Cherry said she didn't think that was such a good idea right now, so I didn't call. It's still rolling around in my head though, like a marble in a pinball machine.

I shared all the information I knew about Dustin with my granddaughter, which unfortunately wasn't a whole lot. I knew he had four girls but I'm not sure of his marital status. I remember Nora thought it was funny that all of his daughters' nicknames were boys' names and she thought it was because he so badly wanted a son. I also remember going over to Nora's when my kids were off from school and there'd be little Dustin, naked on the floor in front of the television, playing tug-o-war with himself. Nora always looked at him and laughed. Even though we were the best of friends, we had contrasting lifestyles and raised our children differently.

Nora was a full-time nurse and enrolled all her kids in a private school that accommodated her unrealistic schedule. If she was on-call and worked a solid ten days straight, her kids attended a twenty-four-hour-school-and-care facility on those days. When she was off, they were home with her. She made good money and could afford the luxury. Nora was never the marrying type (although she was lucky to receive child support for all three of her kids), and I think all her kids followed her example. I don't remember any of them ever marrying. Kimberly and James, her other two children, never gave her a lick of trouble, but that Dustin, well, he was always two sandwiches shy of a picnic and more trouble than a tall mound of fire ants.

Before Gene and Cherry left tonight, they asked me if I'd like to go with them on a dinner date to meet Dustin. My water works started right back up when she asked me and the dam broke. I just wish that Nora could be there. Maybe somehow she will be.

Day Forty

Pop once told my oldest brother that the most valuable thing a man could own was his good reputation. He said it was the one thing that meant more than a fancy new suit or all the money he could carry in his pockets. Respect yourself and others. Be honest. Be trustworthy. Always be fair and generous. I was hiding up in the hayloft when I overheard this conversation, but I grabbed hold of his words as if they were a true pirate's treasure. My father believed that everyone was born with a moral compass and that some folks just didn't choose to use theirs. As I'm writing this I'm not sure if we're really born with a compass or not; however, I do believe that most people learn by example and once the fire log of good starts to burn within them, they just know their way to right and wrong.

Poor Cherry is wrestling with the reason her mother had an affair and because she is confused by it all, she's thinking that Peggy must have purposely meant to hurt her. I honestly don't think that's the case here at all. I think my daughter got herself caught up in some uncontrollable situation and smack dab in the middle of it, she realized it was all spiraling out of control; moving in a direction she didn't want to go. Life does that sometimes. It's a little like that moment of confusion when I wake up from a nap in the middle of the day and I don't know where I am or even the day of the week. It takes a moment to orient myself and get back on track. I'm going to do the best I can to help my granddaughter through this ordeal and I hope to keep her relationship with her mother intact. Right now Brad's tail is thumping loudly on my bed, like an out-of-control metronome and he's staring right through me. I believe this critter might have to go potty.

Chapter Sixteen
"The Silence Was Deafening"

I'd waited a day before sitting my grandmother down and telling her about Dustin because I have to admit that at first, it all felt like a giant conspiracy. I knew how close Granny was to Nora and how much she loved her dear friend and I saw how devastated she was when she lost her. I couldn't help but think that the two of them had to have known about all of this. Maybe they did. They'd been like sisters, maybe closer. When Bert was deployed for six months at a time, Nora spent a lot of time with Granny. When my grandfather died, Nora and Dottie were like Siamese twins. And so it took months for my grandmother to come to terms with Nora's passing. After Granny swore to me that she hadn't known, and with Gene's persuasive force, I decided to make *the call*. Armed with Dustin's address and phone number, courtesy of Gene's sister Jocelyn, I finally found the courage to call and hear his side of this story. Was he even aware that he was Michael's and my father? I just couldn't rationalize any way he could be unaware of not one, but two offspring? How many times had they *"got it on"* for that to have even happened? And where was my dad, Harry, when these trysts were going down?

After three rings, a man answered the phone. He seemed aware of my name and sounded grateful that I'd finally learned the truth. Here is the way our conversation went. The phone was on speaker so Gene could listen too.

Dustin: *"Hello."*

Me: *"Hello, is this Dustin Paul?"*

Dustin: *"Why yes, speaking."*

Me: *"Hi, my name is Cherise Cones and I've recently been given some information suggesting that you might be my biological father?"*

Silence for several long moments.

Me: *"Hello?"*

Dustin: *"Yeah Cherise, I'm here. I've gone over in my head for many years about the words I was going to say if I ever got this call and I suppose I'd pretty much given up at this point and am not as prepared as I thought I would be. I'm sorry for that."*

There were several more moments of silence.

Me: *"I totally understand. This wasn't something I was prepared to hear either."*

Dustin: *"So how are you?"*

Me: *"I'm fine really, just full of questions that I'm hoping you can answer.*

Long pause from both ends.

Dustin: *"Well can you start by telling me what your mother told you?"*

Me: *"Honestly, Peggy hasn't told me anything. I recently found out from my grandmother that I wasn't my father's daughter."*

Dustin: *"Hmm, I wasn't aware that Dottie knew anything about your mother and me."*

Me: *"Well she didn't know that it was you. She only knows that I am not Harold's biological child. I just recently told her, today actually."*

Dustin: *"I see. And what did she say about the news?"*

Me: *"Before or after her seizure?"*

Dustin: (forcing a chuckle) *"Well let's hope she didn't have a seizure. How is she doing by the way? I feel bad that I haven't kept in touch since my mother died. I've just had a lot on my plate the last year or so."*

More silence.

Me: *"Oh, I'm sorry; she's doing great for seventy-six. She's actually a barrel of laughs. So what is it that you do, if you don't mind me asking?"*

Dustin: *"Not at all, but before our conversation goes any farther, I'd like to ask you how you came to find out about me if it wasn't your mother who told you?"*

Me: *"I found some pictures of you and my mother on the beach dated 1976, and since I was born in 1977, several red flags went up on the horizon."*

The silence was deafening.

Dustin: *"Yes, I understand how that could happen. I have a set of those pictures too. I'm surprised Peggy would leave photos out in the open for you to find. She was pretty clear that she never intended to tell either of you about me unless she was forced to.*"

Me: "*Well, you could say that I stumbled across them quite by accident,*" and I felt my face get warm and turn a shade of red as I watched Gene's eyes grow big as saucers.

Dustin: "*So how is your mom doing these days? I haven't spoken to her since my mom passed.*"

Now knowing just how close he lived to my parents' house, I quite frankly found that hard to believe but I didn't call him on it. Some impossible hope sprang up inside me that maybe this ordeal could be worked out really satisfactorily. Maybe Dustin and I could have a relationship, maybe even be friends. My mother would just love that. Not! I could watch her wallow in it though, like a pig in mud. That possibility held some promise.

Me: "*Um, she's not doing so great at the moment. I believe she intended to see this secret die with my grandmother and now that it's out in the open, well, she's not the happiest happy camper.*"

Dustin: *"Well I'm sorry to hear that, Cherise. I realize that this must be a great deal for you to absorb right now, but please know that I've been in love with your mother since she and I were kids."*

A spark came from nowhere and I felt a disturbing fire burning in my belly. I watched Gene's posture become stiff, as if he, too, knew I was about to blow my lid.

Me: *"So if that's true, why didn't you two marry? Why did you sneak around behind my father's back? And why am I just learning that you and my mother have two children together? Did you just do as my mother told you to do? Don't you have a backbone?"*

I took a breath and watched Gene put his index finger to his lips, shaking his head back and forth. He wanted me to take it down a notch and it was all over his face. I thought I'd only grazed the surface. All the questions I'd intended for my mother were rushing out of me like water over a dam and poor Dustin would be drenched, soaked, flooded, drowned, steeped, swamped, saturated, and inundated, if I had my way.

Me: *"And Michael doesn't know yet. He's the lucky one. Right now his whole world is about waiting for my grandmother to pass so my mother can give him a place, a steady home environment, to which he can bring his herd of children two visatation weekends a month."*

I waited but didn't blame him for not responding to my sarcastic tone. I watched Gene's head drop in defeat. He'd given up. I could almost hear the words he would say once the call ended.

Me: *"Hello?"*

Dustin: *"I'm here Cherise, just waiting for you to finish. I didn't have a father when I was growing up, just lots of uncles my mom brought home. I totally understand your frustration with this new situation you've uncovered. I don't blame you in the least. I do, however, hope we can get past it. I'd like to get to know you. I'd like for us to have a relationship. You were my first daughter, only I wasn't given the opportunity to be a part of your life and I want to catch up. You'd have to have known me back when I was young to know the reason your mother didn't want to leave Harry for me. I was the reckless bad boy and she wanted stability. I respected her decision. I didn't really have a choice. Please know that if I'd had the capability to act in a mature fashion, things would have been very different. I just hadn't grown up and Peggy didn't want you and Michael to pay for it."*

I just stood still and listened but nothing else came from his end.

Dustin: *"Cherise, I'd very much like it if you'd come to a barbecue at my house this Saturday. Two of my girls will be there and I'd really like us all to meet."*

Me: *"What time?"* I croaked, in just above a whisper.

Dustin: *"Six p.m."*

Me: *"Okay. May I bring my husband and grandmother?"*

Dustin: *"Absolutely."*

Me: *"Okay, we'll be there. Can I bring anything?"*

Dustin: *"Just you, Cherise. Try to put everything aside and let me meet you."*

Me: *"Okay, see you then."*

Day Forty-One

Well dip me in butter and roll me in nuts. Cherry took me along with her to the grocery store today and I talked her into getting some kale to cook for supper. When I was growing up, my mother fixed us a pot of kale and a skillet full of her delicious cornbread at least twice a week. She loved growing kale because it was one of the few vegetables that she could keep alive in the winter. Both of the kids raised an eyebrow at first but I think once they tried it, they actually liked it. Mine never tastes as good as my mother's did; but isn't that the way it always is? Our fondest memories are ones in which mother is always the best cook.

Cherry mentioned while we were shopping, that she wanted to make potato salad tomorrow and even asked me if I'd help her with the chopping. I believe that child is a tad excited about meeting her biological father this weekend. I have to confess, I am a little curious about it all too. I can't remember the last time I actually laid eyes on any of Nora's children. When she passed, she didn't have a memorial service or funeral. She'd requested cremation and instead of flowers, she requested donations be made to a favorite charity of hers. I was left with no real avenue to say goodbye. I guess that's the part that made losing her even harder for me. Funerals are really for the folks left here on earth, grieving, not for the person passing. I sure miss that gal.

Day Forty-Two

Well toot my horn and blow my whistle, if today didn't beat all. I've already had my evening tea. I've had so much rattling around upstairs I honestly wasn't sure where to begin. I don't believe I've ever felt so many emotions tugging at me in one sitting as I did this day. The kids arrived this morning at their regular time and I didn't bother getting dressed because I was going to get all dolled up later for the barbecue. We spiffed up the house a bit and I received three more Mother's Day cards in the mail, completing my set of five. Because I've been feeling a little run down the last few days, I asked Cherry if she'd let everyone know I wasn't looking for any visitors and I was fine with everyone not making a big deal out of it this year. Maybe we'll throw a big shindig next year. I was looking forward to staying in my bed clothes and watching some of my taped programs rather than entertaining a house full of young ones and their youngsters who surely had better things to do than sit and stare at a wrinkled old prune.

The Sweet Fragrance Floral Shop delivered some beautiful pink roses today from Brock and Amanda. Cherry and I were curious about who this Amanda might be but not enough to go calling and inquiring. We decided to let that dog lie for now. When it was getting close to the time to start getting ready, Cherry laid my clothes out on the bed for me and I went to take my bath. While I was in the powder room, the kids got themselves ready. Gene looked as handsome and dashing as ever and Cherry wore some cute black pin-striped trousers I'd never seen before. Her hair was up on her head and she even wore a smattering of makeup. She really looked prettier than I'd seen her look in a long time. She didn't fuss when she came to see me, so I could tell she really wanted to look special for the introduction to her new-found family. I could feel her excitement running all through me, like the feeling of a roller coaster ride when you're at the top of a huge drop.

After the dogs had all been taken out to potty, we climbed into the car and much to my surprise, Gene acted as our chauffeur. I believe I can count on one hand the number of times I've seen Gene behind the wheel. I figured then that Cherry had to be feeling pretty scattered if she didn't want to drive. When we arrived at Dustin's house, he was out to greet us before the kids even had a chance to get me and my walker out of the car. He plowed right up to me and picked me up off the ground and then hugged me so tight he plumb knocked my dentures right off my bottom gums. When I pulled away and looked at him really close, all I could see was my dear friend Nora in his eyes. The boy favored her something fierce. It actually brought a few tears to my eyes.

When we all got into the house, Cherry got bombarded with hugs from several women who turned out to be Dustin's daughters. Looking at them all together, my granddaughter included, you could see the resemblance to their daddy. I really had a wonderful time and if I hadn't been feeling so tired, I could have stayed forever. As I sat there on the sofa, watching them all scuttling about and happily chatting, I felt as comfy as a cat in a baby's cradle. Maybe I was too comfortable because before I knew it, Gene was waking me up and walking me to the car. I am feeling the weight of this busy day now, so maybe I can continue this tomorrow, when I'm feeling a tad fresher. I didn't even have a cup of Sleepy Time tea.

Day Forty-Three

"You know what makes me really sick to my stomach? It's watching you stuff your face with those hot dogs! Nobody and I mean nobody, puts ketchup on a hotdog!" Clint Eastwood spoke those words in <u>Sudden Impact</u>, *but I was thinking them yesterday when Dustin brought me a hotdog with ketchup on it.*

It was thoughtful of him to wait on me, so I didn't mutter a word and just tried to scrape the red goop off the bun. I like ketchup, don't get me wrong, just not on my hot dogs or hamburgers. Ketchup is for French fries and maybe scrambled eggs *if someone doesn't make them to your liking. Dustin's daughter Charlene, or Charlie as she was introduced, must have seen me wrestling with my hot dog because while I wasn't paying any mind to anything but the dog, I looked up and there she stood with another hot dog. That girl was as quiet as a cat but I thanked her and we switched hotdogs. She asked me what condiments she could bring me and I told her mustard, relish, and some onions. She was a dear and fetched them right away. Then I had another one. I didn't see much of Gene or Cherry; everyone was off chatting and mingling in the backyard, while I stayed perched on the living room sofa.*

Dustin did come to sit with me several times during the evening and we had a chance to catch up on the past. Seems the boy never married; said that Melanie Margarita was the only girl who'd ever stolen his heart. I found that interesting and even a bit heartbreaking at the same time. I told him that he should have straightened himself out and fought for her if that was the case, and he just dropped his head and agreed I was right as rain in springtime. I quickly apologized because he seemed genuinely

The *Second Diary* 197

upset about his failures concerning Peggy, and I realized it was really none of my business. I usually speak my mind about things because biting my tongue hurts like the dickens but I think during this conversation I should have kept my pie hole shut. I asked him if his mom knew about him and Peggy and the two children they'd co-created and again he looked at the floor and shook his head no. That made me so forlorn. I wished we'd known what was going on. When Dustin left me after that chat, I guess I took a little nap because soon Gene woke me up and we headed home. Dustin did tell me at the car that there was something in his mom's attic that he thought she'd like me to have. He asked if he could bring it by sometime and I told him that would be wonderful. Now my curiosity is running rampant and I feel like a kid hyped up on too much sugar. I do hope he calls or comes by soon. Well, I suppose I'll make a cup of tea now; Ryan and I might also share a piece of cherry pie.

Day Forty-Four

This morning the funniest thing happened to me while I was sitting quietly with my first cup of coffee. It's fascinating the way the mind wanders back to the past when a person's least expecting it. I remember words I'd heard my mother say to my pop repeatedly over the years I lived at home and I always wondered about their real meaning. Regrettably, I never found the opportunity to ask her while she was alive, so I still have no idea, but I did manage to come up with a few theories of my own. She'd say, "If you sit by a river long enough, you'll see the body of your enemy float by." When she'd said it to my pop, they both seemed to have a mutual understanding of its meaning but as arduously as I tried, my mind was always unable to wrap itself around a meaning that I could say I understood. Much later I did read somewhere that it was a Japanese proverb and I only discovered that after I read Paul Theroux's book Riding The Iron Rooster and discovered a similar Chinese saying that went like this, "You have to stand on a hillside with your mouth open for a long time before a roast duck will fly into it."

Then while at the library, investigating the origin of my parents' mysterious quote, I came across a charming old Japanese fairy tale, "Mom Taro, the Peach Boy." There are several versions to that tale, all of which I read and loved; the very oldest, a tad on the nasty side. The newest version is simply called "The Peach Boy" and was retold by Gail Sakurai, who muddied the earlier versions with characters from other stories. I remember several older versions though; my favorite ones to read to my children. After never really finding the meaning of the quote my parents had used, I decided to create one of my own, which went along the lines of "If you wait by the river long enough, everyone you've known will eventually float by, even the peach boy." Gosh, I am a silly old woman.

When the kids arrived, I talked Cherry into canceling my appointment for a stress test, telling her that I just needed a few days to build my strength back up. Even the "liquid gold" oil hasn't been helping very much. When I heard talk of a treadmill and hooking me up to some metal tabs, brakes went on in my head, like a train coming to a screeching halt. I believe they lost me at the word treadmill.

Well, Brad and I are thinking mighty hard about having us a left-over- fried- chicken party in the living room and watching a program or two. He never objects to anything involving food. I really like that about him.

Chapter Seventeen
"Aren't We Looking Hot?"

Well, it really was going to happen. Because Gene and my grandmother were over-the- moon excited, I knew there was little chance of me being able to back out now. I'll admit I was a little excited and nervous about Saturday too. A couple of days before Mother's Day, Granny had asked if I'd mind calling my mother, Brock, and my aunts, to ask them not to plan a visit to see her because she wasn't feeling up to it. I agreed to make the calls but not before grilling her to be sure she really was okay. She had seemed noticeably worn out lately, after only short spurts of time; but she assured me that she just wanted to spend the day relaxing, rather than entertaining a house full of family. I got that. I reminded her that we'd be going to dinner at Gene's mom's house but promised to bring her some fried chicken, coleslaw, and biscuits, as well as Gene's homemade cherry pie for dessert.

I also promised to leave Brad or Ryan, knowing full well which one she'd choose. Brad was her favorite, with Ryan following as a close second. She seemed pleased and contented with her Mother's Day plans. I, however, was not planning to see Peggy and when I called her to pass on Granny's request, she was furious when I also announced that I wouldn't be seeing her either. Heather had called and left a message on my answering machine that she and Michael were taking Mom out to her favorite restaurant for brunch and if I wanted to be included, to call her back. I didn't call, for two reasons. First, she knew that Gene and I spent every day now with *OUR* grandmother and second, I felt that if she really wanted me to come, she would have called and spoken to me on my cell phone. The fact that she didn't, made me feel as though she really didn't want me at the brunch; and with my new-found *situation*, that was hunky-dory with me. The way things were left between my mother and me had me feeling as if being apart for a while would really be all for the best anyway.

Before I was able to end our call amicably, my mother all but shouted into the phone, "I hope you remember, Cherise, that I was the one who brought you into this world and raised you, not your grandmother. If you can't find time in your busy schedule to visit your mother on the one day set aside for children to honor their parents, well you're much more of an ungrateful brat than I first thought."

I have to admit I had not seen that coming. I was speechless for a moment. I'm an *ungrateful brat*, really? I inhaled deeply to stop myself from saying what she undoubtedly had coming and replied instead, "Okay," and a small snicker left my lips without my permission. "Tell me how you really feel, Mom. Consider this your Mother's Day call from me. I love you," and I disconnected without further ado.

The day of the barbecue, Gene and I loaded up the dogs along with a change of clothes for the meet-and-greet with Dustin and headed over to Granny's to do our usual Saturday cleaning. I felt it was easier on her if we did things on a schedule, so that she always knew what was happening, rather than feeling like we were invading her space or bossing her around. We'd all sat down together when Gene and I first started coming on a regular basis and decided on a solid schedule we could all feel comfortable with. Everyday activities were written down and posted on the refrigerator each week, so that everyone knew what to expect.

Except for doctors' appointments, we went to the grocery store, cleaned the house, did the laundry, or went out to eat pretty much on the same day every week. I believe my grandmother handled Gene, the dogs, and me being there as often as we were, because she felt as if we were there to accomplish the day's tasks, rather than just babysitting her. Amazingly, it had worked out well, with very few mishaps.

When we arrived at around ten-thirty Saturday morning, Granny was still in her bed clothes, which normally would be a red flag for me that something was up with her but because today was a big day, she was going to get dressed up after her bath and therefore, no cause for alarm. She was just sitting on the sofa, looking happy as a clam in wet sand. Gene and I did our cleaning chores first and then with her in the bath, I went to the spare room to get ready. I'd decided to wear some makeup, which I rarely do, and I put my hair up, only because I thought it made me look more mature.

When Gene came into the bedroom and saw me, he licked his finger then laying it on my shoulder, said, "Sister, whoa! Aren't we looking hot?" and we both laughed.

"Yeah, I want to look hot for my new father, you dork," and I slapped his back as he laughed, fleeing the room.

Suddenly the image of my father, Harry, flooded in. I paused in the room alone for a moment, to allow the reality of it all to register. Was I a horrible person for going through with this? Dustin was probably a perfectly pleasant man but our being related seemed almost ludicrous. Words seemed so inadequate for the flood of emotions I was feeling. Once Granny was ready and the dogs had all been out to potty, we climbed into the car and Gene headed to Dustin's house. The closer we got to his house, the more I could feel my heart thumping in my chest, like a hammer on an anvil.

We had barely pulled up to the curb when I saw someone approaching us from the house. Gene parked and then walked around the car to help Granny. A tall muscular man with unkempt wavy brown hair, which had gray streaks running through it, made a beeline for my grandmother. He lifted her off the ground and did a half- spin, squeezing her tightly. I looked at Gene; his eyes were expressing some concern, but when I looked back at Granny she was grinning like Bozo the Clown. Before setting her back on the ground, he looked directly into my eyes. He looked at me as if he already knew all there was to know about me; as if I were a book he'd already read. It was flipping eerie, like a Rod Sterling flick. When we walked inside the house, my grandmother made her way to the sofa with Gene's help and plopped herself down, where she ended up staying for the duration of our visit. Dustin's driveway was steep and I could tell by looking at her, that the climb had really taken its toll.

Before I'd even taken my watchful eyes off Granny, a woman, in her early thirties perhaps approached us and before I had time to react, her arms were around me in a confining hug. Her shiny brown hair was pulled up into a ponytail that swished jauntily each time she turned her head. I quickly recognized her from Dustin's facebook page.

"Hi, I'm Charlene or Charlie as everyone calls me," she finally said, after releasing me from her hold.

"Well it's very nice to meet you Charlie," I said, reaching for and grabbing Gene's hand. "This is my husband, Gene." and he gave a nod and a smile, "and that sweet old lady over there on the sofa is my grandmother, or Dottie, I guess you'd call her,"

"Well, I'm so happy that you all could come. Two of my sisters will be here shortly" and she peeked out the front window. "In fact, it looks like they're arriving as we speak" and she gave me a smile, excused herself and disappeared out the front door.

Gene raised my hand he was still holding, to his lips and kissed it softly. "So far, so good," he whispered.

Day Forty-Five

All day long I had that darn quilt I made years ago heavy on my mind. I sat straight up in my bed last night after a dream I'd had and it took me forever to fall back to sleep. I dreamed I had embroidered the handprints of Nora's kids in that quilt, along with my kid's hands, and for the life of me I couldn't remember if I really did or didn't. If I were twenty years younger, I'd crawl up in that attic myself. I didn't ask Gene about fetching it again because I was afraid after what happened last time, he might be a little leery about trying it again. The lad does so much for me already. I almost piped up and asked several times today but chickened out at the last second. If I knew right where it was, that would be one thing, but it's been so long now, it could be anywhere up there. I have myself a real quilt quandary. I'll have to give this some more thought tomorrow.

Day Forty-Six

Well, golly gosh and succotash if my prayers about my little problem weren't answered today after all. This morning I'd barely gotten out of bed and sipped half a cup of coffee when I heard a little knock on my front door. I answered it and lo and behold if it wasn't Dustin. At first I was a tad embarrassed about him seeing me all sleepy-eyed and in my bed clothes; but luckily, I can still surprise myself in a moment's notice. I told him that if seeing an old woman in her nightclothes was on his bucket list, he could now scratch it off. He seemed pretty tickled about that and we had ourselves quite a laugh. I did go fetch my robe before offering him a cup of coffee. We had a friendly chat and he gave me a scrapbook his mom had compiled over the years. I thumbed through it and found many pictures of her and me on some of our wild and crazy bus trips. She even had several of our kids at birthday parties we'd had at various parks and pizza places. I couldn't help but smile at all the memories those pictures brought back and then as I closed the book, he said he wanted me to have it. I let loose with a few tears over his kind gesture. I gave that boy a kiss on the forehead and then I had one of my crazy ideas. I asked Dustin if he'd mind crawling up into the attic and fetching the box with my quilt in it and he said no problem, easy as pie. I offered to give him a couple of dead presidents for his trouble and he said that wasn't going to happen. Ten minutes after he'd been up there, he found it.

It was yellowed and dusty but that box was still a sight for sore eyes. "Bless your pea-picking heart," I told him. This old gal was chaffed to bits. Just as he was standing at the front door *fixing to leave, Gene and Cherry arrived. He waved to me and I saw him give Cherry a peck on the cheek before he walked to his car. It seems as if things just might turn out okay for those two after all. I'm pretty tickled about that. Well it's Earl Gray or Lady Gray tea time.*

Day Forty-Seven

The kids arrived today with two big bags of groceries and it wasn't even shopping day. Cherry was acting crazy as a bedbug all morning, smiling, giggling and fluttering about the house. The dogs were acting up too. Cherry would start in the living room and take off running and those mutts would take off after her, around and around the house they ran, like a merry-go-round out of control. Jennifer is by far the fastest; I swear that dog can fly. I about peed my britches just watching them hoot and holler. I waited patiently for someone to share what all of the excitement was about but no one volunteered.

Gene would look at me and then at his wife and say, "Your granddaughter and the children are flossing off for us." That didn't explain a darn thing. She did surprise me with clam chowder for supper though, with lots of extra clams and those little soup crackers I like so much, floating on the top. I do believe it was the best clam chowder I've tasted in years. Then we had fresh sliced pears with caramel sauce for dessert. I'm not sure what's gotten into those kids, maybe buttering me up for something. Whatever it was, we sure had a delightful day. I'm plumb tuckered out tonight. I've still got enough energy to make myself a cup of tea and watch one episode of Jon Stewart before heading to bed.

Day Forty-Eight

I'm beginning to think I have the attention span of a gnat, and a baby one at that. Sometimes my thoughts rattle around in my head with no meaning or purpose. Is that where "rattle trap" comes from? Random thoughts appear as fast as they disappear. One minute something seems important and then poof, I can't remember what I was thinking just a moment ago. Maybe this stage of my life is what old age is supposed to feel like? I don't think that I like it much. Maggie Lou was just two years younger than me and she contracted that memory disease and every now and again I wonder if I might be getting a touch of it too. Then I forget all about it. I have caught myself telling the kids the same stories over and over again but they never call me on it. They're as considerate as a well-trained dog waiting for a treat. Sometimes I think I'm half a bubble off plumb, so I'm sure they've given my sanity a thought or two.

Like today, out of the blue, I remembered the times when I was young, jumping into a big ol' pile of leaves and then being a tad tired and falling asleep in the same pile and my parents having to come find me and wake me up. I remember walking along a creek that ran wild through our property with my two older brothers, and Joe Bob teaching me all about frogs and polliwogs. Then he'd catch a daddy-long-leg in his cupped hands to give me a closer look. I remember my mother's efforts to read an old book to me and make it seem new by doing silly voices for the old characters and the way my dad would recite lines from our books, making us tell him which story he was quoting from. And that he'd made built-in shelves in our bedroom that went all the way to the ceiling and how much fun we had, climbing to the top and jumping onto our beds. We didn't stop until someone yelled, "Mom's coming."

Today all my thoughts have been about how much fun it was being a child and relishing every minute of every day. I guess some days I just really miss my parents. Well, I believe it's now tea time, so as Bronco Bill so eloquently put it, "As our friends south of the border say, Adios Amigos!"

Chapter Eighteen
"A Quilt with Many Pockets"

Dustin had taken the bowl of potato salad from me at the front door and disappeared into another room, leaving us with his daughter Charlie. The front room was beautiful really, full of warm welcoming colors and many homey touches. I realized in that moment, that I had no idea about his marital status. There were a lot of things about Dustin I didn't know. I could see several people in the back yard through the sliding glass door. Everything that happened after that moment really seems like a dream to me now. I was there physically but emotionally I was off in another land. Everyone was congenial, maybe even too friendly. It was all a bit strange. Gene and I made sure that Granny was comfortable and then made our way to the backyard.

Soon we had been introduced to two more of Dustin's daughters, Jolene, or Jo and Samantha, or Sam, as they preferred to be called. Louise, (Lou) wasn't coming. She was out of town and we never really did get any details about the reason why; only that she couldn't be there. Charlie had her two children with her;

Clive, four and Oliver, two. I bent down to introduce myself to the boys and although I'm not big on the whole kid thing, when a two-year-old asks you to have a lick of his Tootsie Pop, you open your mouth. For a kid, he was pretty cute.

Soon Dustin announced that it was time for dinner and I began to make a plate for my grandmother but Dustin stopped me and assured me he'd be happy to do it. Gene and I looked at each other but I allowed him to assume that responsibility.

Gene leaned in and whispered to me, "Good luck with that," as he looked at Dustin and it was all we could do not to laugh out loud.

I guess he must have done okay, because when I checked on Granny, she was sitting happily in the same spot, eating a hot dog. She waved and then shooed me away, so I went back to the patio to visit with everyone. As the evening progressed, the more I listened to Dustin talk about his life, the more I found an astonishing similarity between him and my brother, Michael. Actually it almost seemed as if unknowingly, my brother had molded his life around Dustin's. Neither Dustin nor Michael had ever married, yet they both had children from more than one woman. The only difference between them was that Dustin was settled down in one place and Michael was still looking for a permanent home. I suppose at fifty-nine, one would expect him to *be* settled down. Harry and my brother were never really close, and knowing the truth actually explained a great deal. I'd always thought that fathers and sons were supposed to share some unwritten or unspoken bond. Those two hadn't. The burning question for Gene and me? Did my father Harry know about this behind-the-scenes affair and choose to stay with my mother anyway? Or had my mother kept her secret from him, too? My mind was full of questions, but I was satisfied with waiting for the appropriate time and answers.

As we were all sitting at the picnic table in the backyard, Dustin said, "This potato salad is really delicious," looking down at his plate, "my compliments to the chef" and he looked up at me.

"Well, it's my grandmother's recipe and she told me you liked it because you'd been eating it since you were a kid" and I smiled at him.

As the evening quietly passed, Gene came to me and rather than interrupt the conversation I was having with Charlie's husband, he gestured toward the sofa. There sat my grandmother, head back like a baby bird waiting to be fed, snoring like a seasoned truck driver. We said our goodnights and Gene helped Granny to the car. All in all, it was a pretty great evening. My feelings about Dustin were no longer scary or uncertain.

Now I was focused on Harry and his knowledge of this situation. I'd almost have felt better at that point, if he'd known all along. If he didn't know, well I'd have to give him the loyalty he deserved, in the best possible way. The way I'd pull that off was the real mystery at that point. Things had gotten back to normal with Granny and our routine, until a couple days after the barbecue.

When Gene and I arrived at Granny's, a strange black pick-up was parked in the driveway. Leaving the dogs in the car, we walked to the front of the house and as we moved closer, we could see Dustin standing on the porch, outside her front door. He then threw his hand up and waved to my grandmother and met us halfway down the brick path. He shook hands with Gene and gave me a peck on the cheek before I could stop him; and then he hurried to his truck. Gene gave me a *what-the-heck-was-that-about* look and we went inside to find some answers.

My grandmother was sitting in her favorite spot, still in her night clothes, with a box at her feet. She was grinning something fierce, kind of like a puma with its eyes on the prize. I sat down next to her while Gene went out to the car to bring in the dogs.

"So what was that all about, Granny?" I finally asked.

"Dustin came by with a scrapbook his mom made" and she reached across to the table to pick it up, and placed it in her lap. "And he said he wanted me to have it." I felt my eyes squint together as curiosity overcame me. Picture a cat watching a canary.

"Did he call and tell you he was coming? I'd have thought you'd want to be dressed for company?" and she just sat there with the same Granny-grin, staring back at me.

"No, he didn't call, but it was fine. I asked him to get me that quilt I was telling you about and he found it in the attic, no problem." Her eyes dropped with mine, to the box at her feet.

It looked like whoever had sealed it, used a whole roll of packing tape. Nothing was getting out of that box, for sure, or getting in. It also looked yellowed and very dusty, as if it had been stored for a hundred years. When Gene came in with the herd, Granny asked him if he'd mind opening the box for her and I giggled to myself, knowing the way he'd feel about the layer of dust caked on the top of the box and it being in close proximity to his clothes. I reached down for the box and carried it into the kitchen to wipe it down and cut through the tape, then took it to Granny to open.

Her eyes were wide and lit up like a yuletide fire as she sat looking at the handmade quilt. She asked if I'd spread it out on the floor for her to see and I did, with six little pooches all fighting to be the first one on top of it. It was beautiful. We all ogled at the bright colors that just popped out throughout Granny's work of art and read all the embroidered names aloud.

She was still beaming when she said, "Cherry, reach into one of those pockets and pull out what you find." Not one, but five crisp hundred dollar bills were safely tucked away in the pocket.

She nodded for me to check out the next pocket and I did, until all the pockets were emptied. There was a total of forty-eight hundred dollars, all in one-hundred-dollar bills. Gene and I were in shock. Granny acted unfazed, as if money filled pockets every day. Gene and I had a savings account but we knew to the penny, the amount we had slowly accumulated. I couldn't imagine having that much money stored in the attic of our house. Granny asked me to fold the quilt and put it away in the spare room. She wanted to be sure that Brock received it, and made me promise her that I'd personally see to it. Then she told me she wanted Gene and me to have the money we'd found stashed in the pockets of the quilt.

I looked at Gene. His eyes were huge, his mouth wide open, and I immediately objected. "No, Granny, I'm sure someone else in the family could use this money more than us. Thank you, it's really sweet of you but we're okay."

She patted the seat beside her, for me to sit. She grabbed my hand and gave it a squeeze. She had my attention.

"Cherry, my children are all grown and they're all making their way in life." She quickly moved her eyes to her left and right, as if she were checking the road for oncoming traffic before crossing the street. "I don't see any of my children here, do you?" and she shook her head gently, side-to-side. "No, I see you, Gene, and the wiener dogs" and I smiled as I looked into her face. "I want you to take it. Save it for a trip, maybe a vacation to a far-away island" and I reached for her, gently wrapping my arms around her fragile body. I could feel the tears running down my face and I fought to stop myself from crying vocally.

"I love you Granny," I barely whispered.

"I know you do and I love you too, child," she said.

Day Forty-Nine

The letter I've been expecting from the lawyer finally arrived today. After I checked to see that everything was as I'd requested and when I was sure that no one was looking, I slipped the envelope into Cherry's purse for her to find later. That way, at least one of us will know where it is. It was a heavy weight lifted from my shoulders. Now I have no worries about anything. Life is good.

Heather called me this afternoon to tell me all about the activities in which her kids are involved. She home-schools them, so it's always a certainty that there will be an orchestra of screaming children in the background whenever she calls. She used to phone more often until I was honest about how I feel about the choices she and Jackson were making. I suppose her feelings were hurt when I didn't agree with the many excuses she tried to shove down my throat about the different things her husband was shoving down her throat. She chose to be gullible and accept his excuses and when I called them on it, I believe her feelings got a tad hurt. I won't apologize for thinking that a man shouldn't be allowed to talk his way out of providing some kind of stable income and medical care for his children but that's just me. As old fashioned as a Model T.

Speaking of "T," it's tea time already.

Day Fifty

Last night I woke straight up in my bed from an incredibly vivid dream. It's still lingering in my mind as I write about it now. I don't recall all of it, but I do remember most of it, especially the end. I was under a giant oak tree with a picnic basket sitting on a red-checkered blanket. Butterflies and ladybugs were everywhere, flying freely around me. I could see two distinct paths from where I was sitting. The first path was all in black and white as well as shades of gray. It got darker and darker, the farther my eyes could focus. It looked like a long corridor with the light fading. It was pitch black at the end.

The second path was filled with brilliant hues, all resembling bright Play-Doh colors, gleaming and cascading brightly, as though they were somehow illuminated with flashy clusters of glitter. I tried to stand up to investigate both paths, only to collapse each time I tried to move. I was frozen and all control of my limbs had failed me. I couldn't do anything but sit helplessly and watch everything moving, frame-by-frame, like an old moving picture show, unable to control my reality. I could see all my kids and Bert on the black-and-white path. They were walking slowly away from me, toward the solid black hole that I could only guess was the end. They weren't sad or worried, their movements were more mechanical than human and they weren't showing the fear that I was feeling for them. I could see my mother and Nora at the entrance of the second path, cutting wildflowers and placing them in big wicker baskets. My mother was young and Nora was the same age as she'd been when she passed. I found that odd but I suppose I was just so grateful to see them. I didn't take the time to analyze the meaning immediately. A bird flew anxiously above me and dropped an envelope, sealed with a wax stamp in the shape of a clover leaf. I was able to grab the letter but just as I began to open it, a strong wind caught hold of it and carried it away from me and it landed at the entrance to the first path. No one was there to pick it up. The kids and Bert were already too far down the black-and-gray corridor. For some reason panic filled my chest and I woke up gasping for breath. It all makes no sense and yet I feel as if I was supposed to learn something from that dream. I'm actually worn out just thinking about it all again. Maybe some warm milk would be a soothing change tonight.

Day Fifty-One

I had one of those senior moments today, or brain farts as Cherry calls them. I picked up the phone to call Raylan and halfway through his number, it hit me that no one was going to answer. At first I laughed at myself and then I ended up crying. I hung up but I'm thinking now that even hearing his dead wife's voice might have been comforting. I feel like a silly old fool. I did speak to him anyway; I just rattled off and spoke as if he were sitting next to me. Maybe he heard me and maybe he didn't, but it sure wasn't for lack of trying on my part. I miss that old codger. Cherry asked me which day I'd be up for that darn stress test I'd talked her into rescheduling. It's a funny thing what a dash of pepper in the middle of several sheets of tissue can do. After holding it to my nose and several good sneezes later, it's amazing how convincing my eyes were in my efforts to get my granddaughter to re-schedule my appointment. It worked like a charm. I haven't lost the touch.

Chapter Nineteen
"With No Off Switch to Push"

When we arrived home from Granny's, Gene let the doxies into the back yard and I fished the cash Granny had given us out of my purse and spread it out on the kitchen table. Forty-eight crisp one-hundred-dollar bills look pretty impressive. Gene sneaked up behind me and circled his arms around me, giving me a tight hug and we both just stood looking at the pile of money until he suddenly released me and broke out singing "Gonna Fly Now", mimicking Rocky Balboa's iconic scene on the steps of the Philadelphia Museum of Art. He jumped up on a chair, his arms waving above his head, as he skillfully ran in place. I just looked up at my prince charming and his classically handsome face. It was definitely his laugh and his sexy smile that always did it for me; I was the bowling ball rushing toward the pins.

We burst into laughter as all the dogs began howling at the back door, as they usually did when a fire truck with a howling siren went roaring by. They wanted to be included in our little party. Gene jumped down, kissed the tip of my nose and took a couple steps backward to open the door. I sat down at the table and within seconds was covered with wieners fighting to be the one to reach the throne of my lap.

Gene sat down across from me and looked me square in the eye before he spoke. "Cherry, this was totally awesome of your grandmother. We should put this away and actually *go* to Hawaii and do some island hopping like we've always wanted to. We can afford to pay someone to stay here with the dogs and we can spend two weeks alone on beaches, naked, with no worries, just you and me," and he flashed another one of those endearing smiles, the kind he gives me after we make love.

I hesitated for a brief moment, then heaved an exasperated sigh, "I guess so; if you really want to go, we will," and he grinned wickedly.

As I returned his smile, the doorbell rang and I lifted Ryan from my lap and plopped him on the floor. Gene and I stood and then six excited weenies followed us to the living room. Gene peeked out the peephole as I stood by, anxiously waiting for his report.

"It's your brother and he looks messed up," he said.

I swung open the front door and there stood Michael, eyes swollen and nose bright red as if he were Santa's lead reindeer. He stormed past us without a word and almost threw himself down on the sofa. Gene herded the dogs to the kitchen and locked the kiddie gate, trapping them all in one room. My brother was clearly in no mood to be bombarded with doxie kisses. I sat down in a chair across the room and looked at him, wordlessly. I knew what he was going to say before he even opened his mouth. He'd been told. The way he'd been told I wasn't sure, but his demeanor mirrored the feelings I'd experienced when I first found out about my real father. Like a silent black-and-white film, I watched as a volcano erupted inside him, ready to spew hot, red lava for no particular reason. With no off-switch to push and no handrails to hold onto, I watched as Michael tried to compose himself and speak rationally.

He shifted irritably in his seat. "Mom just blew dad and me out of the water, we felt like a couple of gorged fish. She said you already know. Thanks for the heads up, Cherise. Why didn't you tell me? Hearing it from you would have been way easier, I might not have let my blood pressure go through the roof."

Before I could answer, Gene interjected, "Dude, we just found out ourselves and honestly, it wasn't our secret to tell. Your mom owns it and it's not fair to lay the guilt on your sister like some pouting teenager. If you're upset, keep it where it belongs" and he sat down on the arm of my chair and breathed a bit more slowly.

Moments passed and we watched Michael's anger slowly dissipate; almost melt into the sofa around him as he reined himself in. "Whatever," he said finally. "You're right and I apologize for barging in here all pissed off, but I've just had an exasperating morning."

"Totally understandable," Gene answered, unfazed by my brother's noticeable change in behavior, "but keep in mind that Cherry's world was turned upside down and inside out too. She didn't go to *your* home and take it out on you," and I bit my lip, knowing he had chosen his words carefully.

My brother didn't have a home. He was patiently waiting for my grandmother's house, the result of my mother's devious collusion.

"If it's any consolation to you Michael, I've met Dustin and he's not a bad guy. He was hurt in all of this, too. Mom never gave him a say in any of it either."

His face screamed that that wasn't any consolation. It said his world had just been blown up by an unexpected bomb blast and it was going to take a lot of time to recover from the wounds. He stood and walked briskly to the front door. Gene and I sat like statues, staring sympathetically in his direction. "I'm sorry I said anything," and we watched as he faced the open door to finish the last of his words. "I watched dad leave the house with a suitcase and clearly I should have waited until I'd had more time to digest this news before I intruded here. For that, I apologize" and he never turned back to look at us; he just slammed the door behind him. Seconds later, we heard his tires peel out of the driveway and continue down the street.

Gene grabbed my hand and gave it a gentle squeeze. "Well, that went better than it could have," he said with a determined cheerfulness.

"Yeah, it went just great" I replied.

Day Fifty-Two

Golly Gee Willikers, my grandson called me today. Michael said he'd like to come by and visit with me before I move, and I wanted so much to stop him and tell him that I may look like cabbage, but I'm not quite as green. I didn't though, because I wasn't completely sure how much he knows about what's really going on. I considered the possibility that he's merely an unknowing victim of Peggy's mission plan. I told him to come over and he agreed to visit tomorrow.

I spoke to Cherry about my conversation with her brother and she told me that he'd paid her a visit too. She also said Harry had moved out of the house and was staying at a motel for the time being. All of this mess is a humiliation for everyone involved. I wonder how my daughter envisions it will all end. Maybe she's been living with fear about this happening all along. Secrets can be nasty little boogers and once they're stuck on something, they're hard to shake off. The only secret I can think of that I'm still holding under my hat concerns some bodies I buried under an aged oak tree in the backyard of the old house we lived in before we moved here. I wonder if the new folks ever uncovered those corpses. I suppose I should've come clean about it before they ever bought the house. I'll have to ask Cherry what she thinks about this matter tomorrow. Well, it's bedtime for this fair lass.

Day Fifty-Three

"Well," Clint Eastwood said, "that man's got to know his limitations," and that goes for this old gal, too.

I had some kind of spell today that left me feeling all clammy cold and fiery hot at the same time, like an ice cube melted over fire. Cherry wanted to take me to the emergency room, but I convinced her that I'm an old woman and some days are just better than others.

I tried taking the sheets off my bed by myself before the kids arrived and I did manage to get everything into the washing machine and start it on my own. It just took more out of me than I figured it would. Then I visited with Michael and that went well, but Cherry finally had to run him off, because she thought the boy was never going to leave. Gene kept dropping hints that it was getting late but Michael wasn't picking up what Gene was putting down.

We had Mexican take-out for dinner and while Gene was gone to pick up the food, I sat with Cherry and told her all about the fibs concerning childhood pets when the kids were growing up. I'd told them that their blue parakeet had accidentally flown out the front door and was safe somewhere up in the oak tree in the backyard. Mr. Blue was our first bird, and had actually gotten his head stuck in his swing and died sometime during the night and as luck would have it, none of the children noticed it until they returned home from school. I buried the tiny bird under the tree before school let out for the day and opened the cage door real wide, to corroborate my story. We had many birds and hamsters after that and they always flew away or scurried off; never did any of them die. At least that's the story I told the kids. I could never bring myself to leave them feeling sad or upset about one of their beloved critters. Cherry assured me that keeping all those bodies a secret would be just fine. She said there was no reason to upset people's apple carts now. I'm sure she's right. Tea time is here already.

Day Fifty-Four

Cherry and I butted heads a little today, like two bulls wanting to be heard. She wanted to call her mother and clear some things off her chest; only I could tell she was a tad too upset for that call to be constructive. She's not spoken to Peggy since finding out that Harry had moved out of the house and after hearing what Michael had to say yesterday. She had everything festering inside her like a pus pocket ready to pop. I told her just to let it go; to take the high road, where there was much less traffic, but I could tell she wasn't having any of it. While she sat on the sofa stewing like a pot of prunes, I told Gene that if he'd make us both a cup of hot tea, I'd sweep all the floors in his electronic store. I did get a chuckle out of them and Cherry seemed to calm down some. I told her I was not at all worried about any retaliation from Peggy and that I was positive I wasn't going anywhere. I believe Cherry's head was in a better place by the time they left for home. I'm sleeping with Mr. Brad Pitt this fine evening. How many seventy-six-year-old women can say that? As they say in the Marine Corps, Ooh-Rah!

Chapter Twenty
"The Loudest Fart I Ever Heard"

I'm not certain when she did it, but sometime over the last several days Granny had slipped a letter into my purse. It was addressed to her with a return address from a local lawyer and it had been opened. After closer examination and weeding through the legal jargon, I knew it was some kind of amendment to her present will and looked like maybe a change in her burial arrangements. I showed the letter to Gene and the only thing he could manage to offer me when he finished reading it was "Hinky." I looked at him intently. I was really hoping to hear his thoughts about why she'd given the letter to me to begin with. What was I supposed to do with it?

"She was sending you a message," he said. "She knows you've been concerned and it's her way of letting you know that Peggy can't touch her," he grinned.

"Why do you say that?" I asked quickly. I watched him drop the folded letter on the kitchen table.

"She just can't. Like M.C. Hammer can't," he said with conviction.

I sat back in my chair, arms crossed and glared at my husband. I wasn't in any mood for his antics.

He noticed my displeasure. "She obviously gave you the letter as leverage; an antidote for your mother's misplaced allegiance, something you could flash at her if you need to" and he grinned wickedly.

He was probably right, only I wasn't altogether sure of the ammunition my mother now had in her cache of weapons and the authority Granny might have already given her. I needed to give this lawyer, Nolan Gretsky, a call, and have him explain. I would definitely do that tomorrow; we were already running late this morning.

When we arrived at Granny's, Gene gave her the book she'd asked him to order and her face lit up like a string of Christmas lights. She looked at me and said, "I'm happy, happy, and happy. Hot diggity dog ziggity boom!"

She really loved all fairy tales, but especially those from books she'd owned when she was a child. Whenever she shared stories with Gene and me, they were tales about her childhood. She said that children have the most fun in life because they are the most optimistic and believe in things that adults no longer regard as important. She sat reading happily for more than an hour while Gene worked on the inventory report for the store and I chopped vegetables for a meatloaf. It was noon when I went into the living room to ask if anyone wanted lunch and found Granny sound asleep and Gene busy working in the spare bedroom. I tried gently tapping her and after several tries with no response, I became concerned. Jennifer's head was lying in her lap, so I lifted her and set her on the floor and sat down next to my grandmother to continue my efforts.

My heart was racing and I began shaking a little and terrible thoughts were running through my head. "Granny, are you okay?" I asked, gently shaking her knee. Nothing happened; not even a snort. I held my hand up to her face, hoping to feel her breath and when I'd convinced myself I didn't feel anything, I yelled to Gene.

He immediately came barreling out of the bedroom and put on the brakes when he saw me and from the look on my face, I know he presumed the worst. All of us, the dogs included, were frozen; no one moved a muscle. A long minute passed and I caught myself holding my breath and staring into her peaceful face. When I finally looked up at Gene, I noticed a tear had run down the side of his face and my eyes soon began to brim over. All of a sudden, the room perfectly quiet, Granny ripped one of the loudest farts I'd ever heard. Spanks was in his bed across the room and I watched him crane his neck to see what the noise was. Her eyes popped open and I watched them grow bigger and wider as she focused on all of us looking at her with panic on our faces.

"What's going on?" she asked, less shaken than confused. We all just laughed and I gave her a great big hug.

"You, Granny, just scared the livin' daylights out of us," and I kissed her soft rosy cheek. When I looked her in the eye, she just smiled back at me.

"Well I'm truly sorry for that, dear," and she sat up in her seat. "Is anyone else feeling hungry?"

Day Fifty-Five

While the kids ran out to do errands, I decided to give P.C. a quick call. Brock had told me in a letter that Penny's only child, Savanna, had given birth to a son and she'd named him after Bert. We had a most pleasant chat and she was actually watching the baby while Savanna was at a doctor's appointment. She promised me that once the baby got a tad older they'd travel here for a visit. Yes, we had a good conversation, but these days even dialing long distance wears me out. After my call and with the kids still gone, I took the opportunity to take a little nap. We'd had a wonderful pot roast for dinner with red potatoes and green salad. Gene had been our chef. That boy's a real treasure in the kitchen. I might just do a little reading tonight with a cup of tea.

Day Fifty-Six

I've always believed that there's a place for everything and everything has its place. My mother said that often, so I suppose I have her to thank for being so tidy. Bert was just the opposite. He relished seeing all of his stuff everywhere. He got upset with me when I moved his things, putting them where I felt they belonged. I used to think that was a bit funny because as far as everything concerning the military went, he was King Spic-and-Span. His uniforms had to be just right or I was hauling out the ironing board to re-steam a crease. I wish I had a nickel for every uniform I've ironed. Up until today, I've been slipping this diary under my pillow and sliding it in the towel cupboard first thing each morning. I've felt pretty good about that routine until lately. I believe I'll scribble down my thoughts and then put this book away just to be on the safe side. You never know what tomorrow will bring. My mama kept a journal until the day she died and my brother found it open, lying on her chest, her glasses still on her nose, the morning she passed. I don't believe I'm going to follow in her footsteps with my secret tell-all book. From this day forward, I'll put this diary away before I enjoy my cup of tea. Yes indeedy, my peeking diary will be hidden under the polka dots.

Day Fifty-Seven

We had a surprise visit from Harry today. I believe Cherry's mouth fell to the floor when she opened the door to find her dad standing on the porch. They both just stood staring at each other for the longest time, not knowing whether to spit or sneeze. He finally came in carrying that appropriate Marine demeanor, but after Cherry gave him a big ol' bear hug, he melted back into his usual sweet personable self. I've always liked Harold; he's always been good as gold to Peg and the kids. If you only saw him at home in his family environment, and didn't know what he did for a living, you'd never guess in a million years that he was a drill sergeant. Bert used to say that he left his backbone at the base. He wasn't at all like my husband, who lived and breathed the Marines. Bert used to whisper "Semper Fi" to me before we went to sleep and I was so madly in love with the man that I didn't realize I was getting gypped out of a nightly "I love you."

Harry was more like one person with two distinct personalities. Maybe he had good reason for it, I'm just not sure. I am certain that he loves his children and I can tell just by watching the two of them together that he was pleased as punch, and more grateful than mere words could convey to know that his daughter still loved him. The two of them left to have a chat and a cup of coffee while Gene and I stayed behind just as happy as hobos with ham sandwiches to see them together. Harry hadn't known about Peg's shameful shenanigans and it was clear that he was plumb tore up about it. My pop used to say that even a dog knows the difference between being stepped on and being kicked. Harold had been kicked. I hope Cherry and Harold can begin to heal and together recover their former relationship. I'm sure crossing these gnarled arthritic fingers for them. They sure deserve to be happy. Gene made us both a cup of hot cocoa while they were gone and by golly if that wasn't the best hot chocolate I've had in ages. Now I'd like another cup.

Day Fifty-Eight

Gene and I watched a little piece of the local news today while Cherry was at the vet's with Angelina and Spanks. We listened to a clip from President Obama's Memorial Day speech and it really took me back in time. I remember in 1954 when racial segregation was declared unconstitutional by the U.S. Supreme Court, stating that segregation violated parts of the Fourteenth Amendment. It wasn't long after that ruling when all public schools were integrated. I got to thinking about all of the different presidents over my lifetime that I've voted for and all the presidencies I'd lived through. I wish my parents were alive to witness this amazing time in our world. They were adamant about teaching us to be fair to everyone we met and to rise above others' prejudices and just be compassionate people. They taught us all to see the good in the world, and although evil was always there too, we didn't have to invite it into our hearts. I'm so grateful they were my parents. I only hope that one day my children will feel the same about Bert and me.

Day Fifty-Nine

Today I've really felt like the dog that caught the car. My fanny has been dragging all day like a tired old caboose. I just can't seem to get myself to focus on anything. Then there was the headache. I nipped it in the bud before the kids arrived. When the coffee pot was empty, I asked Cherry if she'd make another one when the first round of caffeine didn't seem to be working, and she looked at me for a long moment before asking if I was feeling all right. I assured her I was and pacified her with my best smile. It worked. She agreed to make me another cup but vetoed my full-pot request.

I firmly believe the girl has all the makings of an excellent mother. She assures me that she'd be quite content just being a good mother to her fur-babies, as she lovingly calls them. I'll agree the dogs are mentally less challenging than human babies, but there's still that little part of me that wishes she'd at least have one child. It does scare me to imagine the name Gene would conjure up for the child. It's also crossed my mind a time or two that maybe he just may have a scrotum full of duds and they just aren't sharing that information with anyone. Well dagnabbit if my head hasn't started to pound like hammers smacking me across my temples again. I'd better fetch some aspirin and brew some tea before the pounding gets unbearable. I might catch a little television tonight, too.

Day Sixty

Well today was a really sad day. I almost passed on pulling this diary out for fear I'd start crying all over again. Last night before the kids left, Cherry asked me if I wanted any one of the dogs to stay for a sleep-over and before I had the chance to pick one, Gene pointed to Spanks, still snoozing away, sound asleep in his little bed, oblivious to the other dogs at the door ready for the car ride home. He just looked too comfortable to disturb.

Cherry asked, "Do you mind if Spanks stays with you tonight, Granny?"

I assured her it would be fine. I wish like the dickens that I'd picked Brad or Ryan now. Both Spanks and Angelina just turned fourteen, and while their offspring will be eleven in a few months, the kids often brag at the way the older dogs were like pups because they were surrounded by their younger offspring. Spanks, more so than Angie, looked plumb worn out most days. Rarely does he venture from his dog bed sitting in the middle of the living and dining room floor. He has a terrific view of all the action from that spot. I always felt that out of all the little rug-rats, Spanks was the gentle soul.

I'm not sure of the time because I was watching a taped episode of "Impractical Jokers" that Gene had taped for me, but when the television sound muted as I was speeding through a commercial, I heard Spanks whining. I looked to his bed and he was M.I.A., so I got up to investigate and when I got to my bedroom, the whining grew louder. As I reached my bed without my walker I lost my balance and hit the floor with a thud. While I was down, I saw Spanks huddled in a ball under my bed and I managed to coax the little guy out. He did that G.I. Joe army crawl to me and once I had him securely in my arms, I began to lift the both of us up toward the top of my bed. Spanks squirmed and squeaked while I held him tightly in my arms until we finally tumbled onto the bed. Once I climbed my way up next to him, hugging my arms around the little boy, I turned to my side in the fetal position while he pushed himself close to my chest. We lay there together, his breathing noticeably labored, but he continued to press into my chest with all of his strength. I prayerfully whispered, please don't let this little one die without his mommy, and within seconds I heard him utter his last breath. I lay there with him unable to move but I managed to say a little prayer for him through my tears. Yes, today was an extremely sad day.

Chapter Twenty-One
"Sweeter Than a Piece of Hard Candy"

"I long for the bygone days when things were simple, when anything was possible. I want to travel back to the time when a nursery rhyme spoken in my mother's voice was as sweet as a piece of hard candy."

That's what my grandmother, Dorothy Rose (Nolte) Hughes, told me the day before she passed. That's what will forever be etched in my mind. My grandmother was both simple and complicated all at the same time. She was a rebel for the ones she loved and a terror to those who tried to undermine her. She left Gene and me with all of her wonderful Granny-isms that will never be erased from our minds any more than our joy and experience of sharing in her existence. To know Granny was the equivalent of reading a really juicy biography with a backstage pass to all the behind-the-scenes footage. She was a masterpiece that the world didn't recognize in her polka dot dress. To Gene and me, she was the epitome of *the bomb*.

We wouldn't trade the time we spent with her for any cash amount. Money cannot buy genuine memories or reveal the meaning of true love. Along the way, while accompanying my grandmother on her final journey, I found hurtful fables in my own life that only she could have helped me through with her wisdom, compassion, and understanding. The last three entries of Granny's diary were both personal and private and all three days her messages were written with her heart and directed to her immediate family members. Because of this privacy, Gene and I have chosen not to share them. It was clear that she knew her days were few and I believe she said all she needed to say.

When we found her, Granny's face was peaceful and serene, her hair down and flowing around her body, a book lying on her chest. As she requested, my husband and I accompanied her body to the little town of Truckee where she was born. Her remains were nestled between her mother and oldest brother. Before they closed her coffin, I slipped a fairytale into the pocket of her pink polka-dot dress and kissed her goodbye. As we watched them lower the casket slowly into the ground,

Gene tapped my shoulder gently and when I looked into his eyes, he nodded to me to look over his shoulder. In the distance, maybe a half city block away, stood a woman in a dark peacoat standing motionless. The distance between us was great, but even I could make out who it was, it was my mother. She'd come to watch her mother be laid to rest. I turned back to see my grandmother settled safely in her final resting place and through my tears I had to smile. My grandmother had a magical power about her to make things turn out for the best, even when she didn't try. The fairytale I wrote and put in her coffin was titled *Flying Carpets and a Damsel in Distress.*

"Flying Carpets and a Damsel in Distress"

Once upon a time in a land far, far away, a beautiful and spiffilicious princess was being held captive in a tower by a super bad-to-the-bone evil king. All of the land surrounding the tower as far as the eye could see was nothing but hellacious, angry trees that came to life at night, ensuring that the princess could never be saved or successfully escape. An epic failure would occur if she ever dared try. To make matters worse, the trees were all haters and at exactly twelve midnight every night they hulked out, spilling their havoc throughout the forest until daybreak. Then they returned to frozen statues. As if the trees weren't problematic enough, a five-headed dragon stood between the princess and her freedom. Each head of the ferocious dragon was powerful in its own way and answered to its own name. The first head was "Peg," known to everyone as the root of all evil, the strongest and most ruthless of the five. Then there was Cricket, Penny, Brock, and Peanut, all disgusting in their own unique way.

Princess Dottie, as she was known in her kingdom, had six faithful knights who were all magically turned into red-haired dachshunds at the hands of the bad-to-the-bone evil king on the notorious day of her kidnapping. As the princess was being dragged away, all of her knights, now canines, wailed out to her, "Woof-woof-woof," which, translated from doglish meant, "Kung-fu is strong and magic is powerful, stay strong princess for we will come and save you!" The princess was counting on her rescue by the fearless 'fenders. While subjugated, she was also cruelly being made to wear frumpy, smelly, old burlap bags instead of her usual pimptacular pink-colored ball gowns she so proudly wore back home. An utter sin, a sign of treason, a total disrespect for her swagger, these clothes she was being forced to wear.

Several weeks into her imprisonment the evil king came to her and threatened, "If you do not hand over the riches hidden in your kingdom, I will send the five-headed dragon to eat your six sausage dogs, one-by-one until nothing but their bones are left when you return."

The princess scoffed at the king and ran to the only window of the tower and cried dramatically, "You will never find my treasure you evil, evil man, and I will be rescued, for I am a good egg and good always wins over evil, you'll see," and the bad-to-the-bone king threw his head back and laughed at her. That very same night at exactly midnight the princess was awakened to the sound of howling in the distance. When she ran to the tower window, she saw three flying carpets, each carrying two tiny dogs, soaring toward her at great speed. As excitement filled her heart, she jumped up and down, cheering the little dogs on. Just as they were a stone's throw from the tower, the five-headed dragon lifted itself from the forest and began swinging at the carpets, threatening to harm the six tiny airborne doxies.

The canines on the carpet closest to the princess tossed a little velvet bag to her before diving out of the dragon's reach. The princess caught the bag and quickly opened it, drinking the magic caster-bean oil from the bottle with all her might. Within moments, she became kung-fu strong! Climbing into the tower window, she jumped blindly into the air, trusting that a carpet would surly catch her. Brad Pitt and Ryan Seacrest, while holding their little doxie noses because the princess really smelled, whisked her back to her kingdom, safe from the evil king and the *five-headed dragon. The princess quickly bathed and changed into a comfortable cotton pink polka dot garment and summoned the town wizard to help her break the spell plaguing her six faithful knights.*

After hours of relentless attempts, it was clear to the princess and the wizard that the evil, bad-to-the-bone king's spell was too powerful to be dispelled. Saddened, the princess summoned the jesters to make signs to be placed outside the front door of her castle. The signs read: "BRAVE PUPPIES FOR RENT; CUDDLE BY THE HOUR." To this day, the kingdom is prosperous and still raking in the gold with folks traveling from far-away lands to cuddle the little red-haired wieners. And everyone lived happily ever after.

The End

~ A Note from the Author ~

*In response to many reader requests, I'm happy to announce

there is a sequel to this story.

"Granny's No Angel"

is now available at Amazon.com.

Thank you for allowing me to entertain you.

C. Threadgoode

Made in the USA
Middletown, DE
26 May 2019